MW01134246

Broken Visions

JESSICA SORENSEN

THIS IS BOOK _____3_____ OF

Shattered Promises SERIES

For information:

Jessicasorensen.com

Cover Design and Photography: Mae I Design

http://www.maeidesign.com/

Broken Visions—Shattered Promises, Book 3

ISBN: 978-1497524828

NP DEC 2014

Broken Visions

Series reading order:

Shattered Promises (Shattered Promises, #1)

Fractured Souls (Shattered Promises, #2)

Unbroken (Shattered Promises, #2.5)

Broken Visions (Shattered Promises, #3)

Chapter 1

I'd always thought life was complicated, back when I didn't know there was something other than the human world. But it was a piece of cake compared to the mayhem I live in now. Vampires. Demons. Evil. Possession. I've experienced it all. I barely remember my possession, honestly. Bits and pieces, Alex desperate to save me, me a total bitch, wanting nothing more than to kill him. Which I did. I killed him…

It happens so quickly that I don't have time to process it. One minute my brain is full of haziness where I can only see one single thought—*kill Alex*—and then suddenly I'm free, my heart flooding with emotions.

Pain. Longing. Need. Sadness. I see so many things. Alex and I. Our hide out. Violet flowers. Dancing in a field. Blood Promise. *Forever.* Everything I've ever felt in my past, before my emotions were erased, surges through to me and jumpstarts my emotions.

I scream at the top of my lungs. "*Stop!* Stop! Stop! Stop. It's me. It's me. Alex, stop!"

But it's too late. He gags as he pulls the needle out of his heart. Gasping for air, his skin pallid, eyes wide. Seconds later, he crumples to the floor.

A blood-curdling scream rips from my lips. "Aislin! Untie me! *Please.* He can't die now!" *I did this. This is all my fault. No! Help! Stop. Please. God, it hurts so much.*

Aislin buckles over Alex's body with her head tucked down as she utters a chant under her breath, over and over again. Her hand glows red as she presses it to his heart. I realize she's doing a spell, hopefully one that will bring him back. However, the longer it goes on, the more my hope crumbles. After a while, Aislin gets quiet, tears still falling from her eyes as she looks up at me.

"He's dead, Gemma. He's dead," she whispers softly as the glow from her hand fizzles away.

"No, he's not!" I cry as I tug on the ties around my arms and legs. "Aislin, please untie me. I need to be with him."

She's finally able to get up, then she moves over to me, her eyes swollen; tears streaming down her cheeks. She unfastens the ties around my wrists, her fingers shaking. As soon as she gets the last one un-done, I spring upright and scramble over to where Alex is lying on the floor. His eyes are open, though distant and vacant; his arms and legs are sprawled across the floor. He's not breathing. I check his pulse with my fingertips. Nothing. I try to feel the sparks. Nothing. *I feel nothing.*

I vaguely hear Aislin say something to me, but I can't make out her words. There's so much pain. Hollowness and it's growing larger every second his heart isn't beating. I feel like I'm being pushed down from it. Sinking. Falling. Dying.

***

There's a frozen lake before me and icicles dangle from the leafless tree branches enclosing the water. The dark sky casts a shadow over the icy land and the air is as chilly as death. Alex's arms are wrapped tightly around me as we stand near the edge of the frozen water, holding onto one another as if our lives depend on it.

"We'll be all right, won't we?" I ask him. A breeze gusts through my hair and the silence around us makes the world feel desolate. Yet somehow at the moment, I feel whole; at peace, calm.

I tip my head back and look up at him to tell him my how I feel, but he shushes me as he brushes my hair away from my face. "It will be all right," he whispers, but his voice is unsteady.

My lips part to disagree, because I can feel the omen in my bones, but a crackle rips through the air and steals the words from my lips. Moments later, several tall, cloaked figures with skin of the dead and soulless glowing eyes emerge from the trees and surround us.

"Death Walkers." I look at Alex in terror. "What do we do?"

He pulls me closer to him. "It will be all right," he whispers again, his body heat the only drop of warmth we have left. "Just trust me."

I feel warmth and pain. Heat and agony. Then suddenly I'm suffocated by light. Yet for some reason, it feels like everything will be okay. Gripping onto him, I take a deep breath and let the warming light engulf me and take me away from the world. Then there's a rough tug and I can feel Alex slipping away. I let out a scream, but we lose each other in the light.

***

"*Gemma*," a voice calls out to me. "*Can you hear me?*"

My body tenses as light encircles me. "Who's there?"

"Come toward me," the voice echoes.

I lift my hand to my forehead and try to shield my eyes from the blinding light, but I still can't see a thing. "Whoever you are, I can't see you... The light's too bright."

"Yes, you can," the voice assures me. I'm certain that it doesn't belong to Nicholas, even though it seems like something he would say to fuck with my head. The voice is much deeper, and sounds older and wiser. "You just have to look harder."

I blink a few times and the light begins to dim. Slowly at first, and then more quickly, until there's nothing left other than a soft glow orbing around me. I can see my hands and arms... my feet... I start to get my bearings when, suddenly, my legs are ripped out from under me.

I tumble down a rabbit hole for what seems like forever until, finally, I land on a hard surface on my back. My vision comes into focus and I'm shocked to my very core at what I see. A midnight-blue marble floor, a cathedral ceiling painted with intricate art, and tile walls of sapphire blue and shimmering silver. It's beautiful—too beautiful.

"I have to be dead," I mutter, getting to my feet. I examine myself. My skin is pale, but that's normal, and I can feel the air coming in and out of my lungs, my heart still beating in my chest. I have to be alive, but where the hell am I?

"Hello!" I call out, turning in a circle between rows of columns that lead to a colossal statue.

I head for the statue, taking each step carefully, afraid that any second someone—or something—will jump out from behind one of the columns. Quite honestly, I think I'm hoping Alex will appear from somewhere. Surprise me. Tell me he's okay... that he didn't... die.

I start crying again as I reach the end, thinking about where Alex could be and if he's alive. My heart feels shattered. Broken. I'm broken. Just like the statue with a crack down the center, although it's still intact. Made of flawless, white marble and perfect edges, it forms a figure that looks like a tall man. Looking closer, there is something about the angles of the face that look familiar, and there's a crystal ball chiseled in his hand.

"What in the hell?" I lean closer, squinting at the plaque mounted on the statue's feet. As soon as I read it, my pulse quickens to the point that it knocks the breath out of me. "Julian Lucas. Lucas? No. There is no way." I cover my mouth with my hand and back away. Where am I? What is this place?

"Don't worry, it's just a statue," someone says from right behind me.

I spin around and jump back when I come face-to-face with a man that has a striking resemblance to the statue, only he's alive and breathing. He has shoulder length, brown hair and violet eyes.

"Oh, my God, you're... you're..." I place my hand over my trembling mouth and shake my head.

"Hello, Gemma," he says calmly. "I'm so glad you finally found me."

"But you're... how... why..." I can't form sentences.

Thankfully, my dad understands. "Don't worry. I'm here to help you."

"Help me with what?" I finally get a full sentence to leave my mouth.

He smiles. "Fix the past and create a better future."

I glance around at the strange place I've dropped into. "What do you mean? Where am I?"

"You're in the only place I can be," he says, turning around and putting a hand on my back to steer me with him as he walks down the path.

I move nervously with him, my heart erratic in my chest. "What do you mean by fix the past?"

"I mean, we're going to do what probably seems like the impossible," he says. "We're going to reset time and erase some of the past to hopefully create a better future for the world."

My heart quiets inside my chest. Calms. For the briefest moment, I swear I feel sparks of heat, tiny firecrackers. If what he's saying is true—if we're going to erase some of the past to hopefully help the world—then maybe I can also help Alex.

Maybe I can reset it so he doesn't die.

Maybe I can bring him back.

Chapter 2

As we hike down the path toward the unknown, I watch my father out of the corner of my eye. He looks so much like me; brown hair, fair skin, tall, and of course the violet eyes. It's almost too good to be true and with faerie/Foreseers like Nicholas roaming around, who can turn into a mirage and make me see things that aren't real, I have to wonder if my dad isn't real or nothing but an illusion manifested, perhaps, by my death. Maybe Aislin's mirage protection spell isn't working anymore. *Maybe I'm the one who's dead.*

"Am I dead?" I dare ask.

He shakes his head understandingly. "No, you're fully alive."

I continue to study him; sharp features, a warm smile, confidence in his walk. "Are you dead then?"

He shakes his head, a sparkle in his eyes. "Not quite."

"Is that even possible? To not quite be dead?"

He considers this carefully, gazing off at the columns lining the path. "You're here in your vision form."

15

I swallow the massive lump in my throat. "So my body is still back on earth? Passed out?"

"Yes, pretty much." He pauses. "But don't worry, today isn't the day you're going to die, Gemma. I promise." His silver robe swishes across the floor as the path curves upward, almost as if it's bowing into the sky and carrying us along with it. "We only have a few minutes before you have to return and I have something very important I need to show you."

"Okay." Light glimmers from the ceiling. "Is it how to reset time and bring back Alex?" I half expect him to yell at me, for putting a guy before the world's needs, but he simply nods.

"If all goes well and you're able to pull it off, then yes, Alex will come back too," he says, nodding.

"So this is all in my hands?' I ask. "I mean reset-ting time?"

"You sound skeptical?" He notes curiously as the path dips downward again and I have to work to keep by balance and not fall to my ass and slide down.

I shrug with my hands out to my side. "It's just that I've seen and heard things that make me think that it's not possible to change time. Or that I should."

"You've seen them in your visions I'm assuming?"

"Sort of..." I gape at him. "Wait, you know I can see visions?"

He smiles as we arrive at the bottom of the hill, then we veer to the right down a slender hallway lined with porcelain columns engraved with gold leaves. The ceiling is swirled with various shades of yellow and blue, creating an effect similar to Vincent van Gogh's *The Starry Night*. The place is surreally gorgeous, unlike anything I've ever seen.

"Where do you think you inherited your Foreseer gift?" my father asks as I gaze at the beauty around me in awe. "And, just like you, I have unique Foreseer abilities."

I tear my attention off the scenery and focus on him. "So you can do things besides just see visions?"

"Yes, but that is a story for another time," he tells me with a sad smile on his face as if it'll never happen. "Right now, you need to focus on creating a better future for the world."

I have a ton of questions I'm dying to ask him. It's my first time meeting him, and I want to know everything I can about my mother, my past, him. But there's urgency in his voice that keeps my lips sealed. And besides, deep down in the pit of my heart, most of my attention is on Alex, back at the beach house, dead, something I need to fix. In fact, just thinking about it

17

makes my heart feel like it's rupturing open and bleeding out, but whether that feeling is coming from the star or from my own emotions, I'm unsure.

I bite on my nails and remain stuck in my own head and the what if's as we make the rest of our journey. At the end of the hallway there's a stairway stretching up a sloped floor toward a brick mausoleum. Two massive pillars form an entryway to the heavy wooden door on the front of it where there's a red light glowing from a barred window.

"What is this place?" I ask, hoping that it just *looks* like a mausoleum and doesn't actually have dead bodies inside it.

He doesn't answer as he climbs up the stairs toward the mausoleum. I rush after him, the steps cold underneath my bare feet, making me aware that I don't have any shoes on and painfully hyperaware that I can barely remember anything up to the point where I woke up from my possession and Alex was dead on the floor. This has me worried about what I did while I was under Stephan's control. What if I'm not remembering more evil things I did? What if I hurt more people?

I glance down at my arm where he branded me with the mark, now gone, my skin back to it's smooth, paleness. I remember how Stephan told me that I had evil in my blood and that's why he was able to put the mark on me. What if that was true? What if I do have evil in me? What if this showed terribly when I was possessed? Even if I do manage to reset time and erase it, it can't necessarily erase what's inside me.

"Everything okay?" my father asks, sensing my distant thoughts.

I nod, unsure how to ask if somehow I have evil blood in me. And what if it came from him? "I'm fine... just thinking about Alex... and how he was..."

"I understand," he says. "Losing someone can be difficult, especially if you're not used to death."

I want to say that I am used to death, though. Hell, I grew up thinking both of my parents were dead. But now I've met them both, fully alive and breathing so it's not really relevant. And besides, during most of the time I thought they were dead, I couldn't feel emotions so there was nothing inside me gnawing away like it is now.

"Hopefully, I won't have to get used to it yet," I say with a forced smile.

"Hopefully," he agrees, coming to a stop in front of the mausoleum door. He reaches for the brass handle and the hinges creak as he opens it, as if it had been sealed shut for ages. Then he ducks his head and steps inside the dark and I hesitantly follow.

It takes my eyes a moment or two to adjust to the lack of light and my skin and lungs take even longer to get used to the damp air. "It feels like death in here," I whisper, hugging my arms around myself.

"That it does," my father replies, giving me no hope that this building isn't a final resting place for the dead. He hunches over even more as he begins to descend farther into the dark. The low ceiling drips murky water on our heads and the cold tile floor is cracked and stained. The pillared walls are deteriorating, chipped and flawed, but in a hauntingly beautiful way. Decorated with red lanterns, the whole place has a soft glow which flows around the room and lights the way down a narrow tunnel.

"This way," my father instructs with a nod of his head, reaching up to unhinge a lantern from the wall and carry it with him.

I trail after him, the air growing heavier the further we go and the floor feeling more like ice than tile. I start noticing little details the more my eyes adjust to the dark. The way vines flourish from the ceiling, the sound of a river flowing from somewhere nearby, how on each pillar there is an eye carved in the center, the pupil an *S* wrapped by a circle—the Foreseers' mark. Is this a place for the Foreseers? Is it linked to the City of Crystal? That idea makes me nervous, especially if Nicholas has access to it.

"What is this place?" I trace my fingers along one of the eyes. "Does it have something to do with the Foreseers?"

My father shakes his head, the lantern swinging from his hand. "This is a place where no one wants to be."

I'm about to ask him to explain more, but we reach the end of the tunnel where there's a large midnight blue trunk, trimmed with gold, perched on top of a Victorian table. My father sets the lantern down beside the legs, then raises the lid of the trunk and sticks his hand inside, retrieving a crystal ball orbed with soft light.

He extends his hand out toward me, his violet eyes more dark lavender. "This is how you're going to reset time and hopefully create a better future for the world."

I eye the crystal ball warily. "With just a crystal ball?" I look up at him. "How?"

He takes my hand, his skin alarmingly chilled, and he carefully places the crystal ball my palm. "No, with this and your power."

It isn't like any of the other crystal ball I've seen. The outer glass is crystal clear, allowing me to see inside where a star-shaped center bursts with light.

"I don't understand…." I'm transfixed by the crystal ball, unable to take my eyes off it, as though it's beckoning me to use it. "I thought my power was what ended the world?" I lift the crystal ball to eye-level. "This crystal has a lot of power…"

"That it does." He shuts the lid on the trunk. "And when I say power, I'm talking about your Foreseer power, not the star's power." He stands silently for a moment, struggling to tell me something important. "I've done some things in my life that have led me to this place. Things that are unforgivable—things which you'll understand soon. But I need you to put the future back and fix some of those mistakes."

I wonder if the evil in my blood came from him. "Unforgivable things?"

"I can't answer that right now," he says. "Nor can I tell you how to use the crystal ball."

It fills like I've been stuck in some sort of riddle world, where I have to figure out the answers from a bunch of stuff that doesn't seemed to be linked to anything. "Why can't you tell me anything?"

"Because you have to figure it out on your own." He tries to offer me an encouraging smile. "You and I are unique cases. We can both travel into visions without the assistance of a crystal. With enough strength, you should be able to change the vision I erased and recreated."

I'm dumbstruck, my fingers tightening around the crystal. "You *changed* a vision? I thought you weren't allowed to do that?"

"You're not." Regret seizes his expression. "The vision I changed was so the world would end... And to this day, I regret it."

Evil. Evil. Evil. The word echoes in my head. "You made it so the world would end? How...why would you do that?" I step back. Maybe he's still evil and he's getting me to do his evil work.

"Relax, Gemma. I assure you there are good reasons for why I did the things. Granted, it's not an excuse, but at the time it seemed like it was the only option."

I back away until my back brushes the wall. "There are no such things as good reasons for doing something evil." I shake my head, feeling the ache of another hidden wound.

"You've never done anything bad that felt like it was the only option at the time?" he questions with accusation.

I open my mouth to say no, but deep down I know it's a lie. "Yes, but..."

"No buts. This isn't important right now." His voice is startlingly sharp, his hands balling into fists, anger controlling him. "What's important is that you fix it— change everything back to how it was originally sup- posed to be. You need to make sure the world doesn't end up like it did in the vision you saw."

I shiver as the images surface, the one's I've seen of the world in its icy demise. "The one where the world ends in ice—the one where Stephan and De- metrius and the Death Walkers win?"

He relaxes a little. "Yes, that's what you need to stop from happening."

I want to argue with him more, but there's a voice in the back of my mind reminding me that if this works correctly, I'll have Alex back. I see the bigger picture of what my father was talking about and it makes him seem less evil, or me slightly more—I'm not sure.

"Alright, but you need to tell me what to do, be- cause I have no clue," I say, moving back toward him.

He taps the crystal ball I'm holding with his finger. "Everything you need to know is in here." He places his finger to my temple. "And in here." Then he turns his back on me and starts to walk away. "It's time for you to go back. Good-bye, Gemma. I have great con- fidence that you'll be able to fix my mistakes."

I start to chase after him, desperate to know more, but the walls around me bow in and out and the entire room starts to spin and becomes distorted like a funhouse. My knees lock up on me and I can't move. My father walks further away from me and the tunnel begins flickering in and out of focus. I attempt to run after him again, wiggling my legs and arms and putting all my strength in it, but he just keeps getting further and further out of reach.

"But I don't understand any of it!" I shout, clutching onto the crystal ball. "How am I supposed to change visions if what I've been taught is that they're not changeable? And how do I know which ones to change?" I stop fighting, my feet heavy like bricks, and I'm submerged by darkness. "Dad, I don't understand!"

"Don't worry." His voice seems to come from everywhere. "You will."

Before I can say anything else, I'm being flipped upward and tossed into the darkness.

Chapter 3

Cold water splashes across my face and over my body, soaking my skin and my clothes. My body feels like it's been ran over by a truck and my eyelids are so heavy it aches to try and open them. The air smells salty and is filled with the soft lull of the ocean. For a while, I just lie there, trying to decipher what's going on because I'm too exhausted to move. But when water crashes over me again, I open my eyes just in time to see another wave headed at me. I scramble to my feet, hacking up water as I race up the beach and out of the ocean's reach. I can't believe what I'm seeing. The ocean before me, sunlight reflecting against it, and behind me, houses and people basking in the sand. I'm back at the beach house in Maryland.

I would think that what had just happened was a dream, but I'm still clutching the crystal ball my father gave me.

"I'm here, which means..."I sprint off for the beach house where Alex, Aislin, Laylen, and my mom are, at least from what I can remember. I'm just hoping that it worked—that I'm back to a place in time where Alex is alive, I'm not possessed and everything is good, well as good as it can be.

I make it to the house in record time, panting, sweaty, but feeling better than I have in a while. I barrel up the stairs of the back porch and fling open the screen door. "Mom," I yell, stumbling into the kitchen. "Mom! Alex! Aislin! Anyone!"

Silence.

I hurry from the kitchen to the living room, calling out everyone's names, but the only noise comes from a grandfather clock in the corner of the room next to the sofa. Where is everyone? Did they go looking for me? Or did it... God, no I hate to think it, but I can't help it. My father gave me very little details on how this would work which makes me wonder if maybe Alex is still dead or something and that's where everyone is.

After searching the entire house and not finding any clues to where they could be, I begin looking for a phone. But then I realize I don't have anyone's number so it's pointless. I'm about to endeavor out and start searching the streets when the front door opens and Alex enters, breathless. His dark-brown hair is messy, like he'd been raking his fingers through it repeatedly. His green eyes are wide and his lean muscles look taut through his T-shirt. His lips... God, his lips look so kissable.

The sight of him nearly sends me to the floor, my heart slamming against my chest so forcefully I can't think. "You're alive," I breathe, gripping onto the end table to support my weight.

He gives me a strange look, stopping just short of me. "Of course I am…" His brows furrow as he reaches out and his fingers spread across my cheek. Sparks ignite. Dance across my skin. Elated. Alive. "Are you okay? You look like you're going to be sick," he says.

"I think I am," I tell him, still stunned. Because my father did it. He reset time. He brought Alex back…

All I want to do is touch him. Feel him. Run my fingers through his hair, along his arms, his muscles, feel the smoothness of his skin. I want to taste his lips. Let his lips taste every inch of me. But Stephan's words echo in my head, the consequences of us being together.

When Alex moves to touch me with his other hand I step back, even though it nearly kills me.

"What's wrong?" he asks, confusion swarming across his face.

He has no idea.

How can I tell him? How can I tell the one person I've ever felt anything for that our emotions we have toward each other are wrong. That this amazing chemistry we have was never meant to be—that we were never meant to be.

"We can't..." I shake my head, my stomach burning. I swear to God telling him is what's going to end me. "We can't..." *I can't do this.*

Tears sting in my eyes, the knot in my stomach winding tighter. Blinding white heat ignites from inside me, so potent and toxic it feels like I'm on fire. The prickle appears, invisible but equally as toxic, piercing at my skin, telling me something I can't interpret just yet, or maybe just don't want to.

"I can't breathe..." I choke. *What is wrong with me? Something's not... right...* I collapse to my knees, my fingers digging into my chest. "I... can't... breathe..." As I struggle for air, my vision spotting in and out, all I can think is, *I'm dying.*

The next few minutes pass by in a blur. Alex rubs his hand up and down my back, whispering soothing words. *It's going to be okay. You're alright. Just breathe.*

Just breathe.

It's hard to breathe through the crushing ache in my lungs, my bones, everywhere. But after he gets me to the sofa and sits me down, I lower my head to my lap and take deep inhales and exhales, my heart starts to beat steady again and oxygen returns to my lungs.

I sit up with my arm wrapped around my stomach, blinking as the blood rushes from my head. "What happened?"

Alex is kneeling on the floor in front of me with his hand still on my back, eyeing me over with concern. "I think you were having a panic attack."

I shake my head and scratch the spot of skin on the back of my neck where the prickle is going wild, the area a little tender. "It felt like I was being smoth- ered."

He moves his hand from my back to my leg. "Pan- ic attacks can feel like that…" he trails off considering something. "But what I'm wondering is what hap- pened to cause the panic attack? Is it because Laylen's still missing?" His expression slightly hard- ens. "Because I promise we'll find him. You're mom and Aislin could have found them already too and just haven't made it back yet."

Sparks dance recklessly across my skin, remind- ing me of everything we are and never can be. "Find Laylen? Is he missing…" It dawns on me. I went back into the point in time where Laylen ran off, but I was never captured by Nicholas.

"Gemma, what's wrong? You look like you're going to be sick?" Alex skims over my body, assessing every part of me, making the sparks more intense and the consequences of them even heavier. "And why are your clothes wet?" His eyes drift to my hand still clutching the crystal ball, our fingers brushing and sending a surge up my body. He takes it from me and rotates it in his hand. "Where did you get this?"

Without even thinking, I extend my hand out and place it on Alex's arm. The electricity surges with contact. I stare at the window over his shoulder, the sunlight blinding but refreshing in the best way possible. "I can't believe it worked."

Alex gets to his feet then sits down beside me with a concerned look on his face. "Gemma, I don't know what's going on but I'd really appreciate it if you'd explain it to me." He's trying to be patient with me instead of his normal, bossy self, probably because recent information about his father and what he did to all of us, including Alex himself, is affecting him.

"Something happened to me," I tell him. "But I'm not sure if you're going to believe it or not."

His brow arches. "I'm not really sure there is anything I wouldn't believe at this point."

He has a point. So many crazy things have happened over the last week or two that it makes anything seem possible, but still, everyone has been telling us how changing visions is impossible and I just reset time. I need to explain everything to him and I mean everything, not just about resetting time, but what led up to the point that it had to happen, which means telling him about Stephen and my possession and the worst part—how we're not supposed to be together. How we can kill one another if we fall in love. But before I divulge this to him, before I give *him* up, I want him one last time. The prickle hasn't announced my love for him, or anyone else for that matter, yet and I'm not sure if it ever will, but what I do know is that Alex will more than likely put a stop to all the touching, kissing, cutting off the human contact I've been deprived off for years and I want it one more time before it's gone.

So before either of us can say anything I lean forward and press my lips to his. I try to shut down the overwhelming heat, the passionate sparks, the scorching hot desire that tidal waves through me as I slip my tongue into his mouth.

He kisses me back without any hesitation, as if he has no control over the situation or anything else, and honestly, I don't think either of us does. We're prisoners to our lust, want, need, a million different things that feel like they own me all the damn time and I'm giving in.

"I surrender," I say against his lips, not really too him.

But he pulls back, eyes glossy, filled with desire, an addict wanting his next taste, just how I feel at the moment. "Huh?" He cups my cheek. "Gemma, please tell me what's wrong."

I want to tell him, but not yet. The greedy addict in me wants just one more moment before I give it all up. "I surrender," I say again, like it's supposed to mean something, and the flash of hunger in his eyes makes me think that it might mean something to him.

Suddenly he's colliding his lips against mine and everything that matters doesn't. Nothing else exists.

Nothing.

Out tongues tangle together, hands wandering all over each other's bodies. I forget how to breathe like I did seconds ago, but it doesn't matter. Let me stop breathing, because that's how it's going to be in a few minutes. As the excruciating pain of reality bares down on me, I suddenly get to my feet. Alex starts to protest, but I grab his arm and pull him to his feet. Then before I can stop myself, I move to tug his shirt off his head, but somehow in the intensity of the moment, I manage to rip the fabric in half, as if I've gotten stronger somehow. Alex looks down at his chest, shocked, and I feel the same way. But the shock fizzles as I take in the sight of his flawless muscles and fiery sun tattoo blazing on his skin—his Keeper's mark—and instead I trace my fingers along it, noting how fast he's breathing.

His gaze lingers on my hands, and then drifts to my face. Something in his eyes causes heat to coil deep inside me and course through my veins like a powerful drug. He wants me as much as I want him and it nearly sends me through the roof. I'm about to smash my lips against his, unable to control myself, but he stops me, reaching for me. And like I did with him, he tears my shirt from my body, but with purpose unlike me. Then with one swift movement, he has my bra undone and moments later we melt together like liquid steel.

I slip my fingers through his hair and tug on the roots, causing him to moan and start backing us up somewhere. Clothes come off on our way down the hallway, pants, boxers, panties, most of which gets torn to shreds. My nails scratch at his skin, claw at his back, as he bites at my lips, my neck, groaning over and over again, leaving teeth marks on my body that leave a wonderful ache along my skin. The twisted part of me hopes they'll leave scars, that way I can at least have a reminder of this when I'm full of emptiness again.

We continue to kiss and tear each other apart, never making it to the bed. Instead he picks me up as soon as we step into the nearest room and slams me into the wall so hard I'm sure I'm going to have a bruise. But I don't care—I don't care about anything at the moment as I fasten my legs around him, allowing him to rock his hips and thrust deep inside me.

"Oh God." My head tips back and I moan louder than I ever have as my fingernails dig even deeper into his flesh, cutting it open and causing blood to trickle out. Thankfully he's a Keeper, otherwise he'd have scars all over his body. I wish everything was that way—that if we were strong enough we'd escape getting scars, outside *and* in. Maybe then I could erase the scars of life. Maybe then I would know that when this moment is over and I know I can't have it anymore, my heart and soul won't be scarred.

But I know that's not the case. I realize as Alex kisses me, slipping in and out of me, touching me more than anyone ever has, that I feel more for him than I'll ever let myself admit.

Then I ever can admit.

Chapter 4

After we both come together, we relax and finally make it to the bed. Naked. Sweaty. And exhausted. Alex is lying next to me, one hand to his side, the other in his hair as he smiles contently at the ceiling. I lie on my side and stare at him, the elation and bliss he instilled inside me rapidly dissipating.

"That was…" he searches for words, catching his breath.

"Amazing," I finish for him only my deflated tone doesn't match my word.

He picks up on my depressed vibe and frowns at me. "What's wrong?"

I shake my head, trying to keep my lips sealed, telling myself that it's okay to keep the secret just a little bit longer. But suddenly my conscience takes over and everything comes spilling out. Everything that happened to me over the last few days, or didn't happen anyway, but I dither around the most major revelation of all, at least when it comes to us.

When I finish, Alex eyes are enlarged, his mouth hanging open, flabbergasted. "So what you're saying is that right now we're technically in the past."

I prop up on my elbow and rest my cheek against my hand, ignoring how his gaze sweeps across my naked body and causes my skin to swelter. "I don't think so. I think the days I spent possessed have been erased since I can remember them. I think that maybe somehow my father erased and recreated some of the events of my life, so that I would end up back here in this point of time… with you… fully alive." I move to pull the sheet over my body, but Alex snags my hand and stops me.

He bites his bottom lip, reflecting. "And so that my father never got a hold of you and you were possessed?"

"That too." I blow out a tense breath, knowing I'm going to have to tell him the rest soon. "He told me he erased a vision once and recreated it to change the outcome of the world's future… changed it so that the world would end the way I saw it in my ice vision." Tears sting at my eyes. When my father had told me, it didn't seem as bad, but I think I might have been in some kind of semi-subdued state, or shock, because now it is really kicking in and I feel like I'm about to lose it.

"Hey, we'll figure this out." Alex brushes a strand of my hair out of my eyes. "Everything will be okay. I promise."

"I know, but my father… I just can't believe he did that." I suck back the tears. "And he's trapped at that place."

"Where exactly was he?" he asks, resting his hand on the curve of my hip.

"He wouldn't tell me exactly where he was. He wouldn't tell me anything really, other than I have to save the world somehow. And that everything I needed to know about saving the world was inside in my head and that crystal ball."

Alex massages my hip absentmindedly. "It's so strange, though. I've always been told that Foreseers aren't supposed to control how the future turns out or recreate visions how they want them. They're just supposed to *see*—not touch."

"Yeah…but I don't know…it seems like it could be possible. I mean, look at me. I can travel around wherever I want by using my Foreseer ability, without the aid of a crystal ball, which isn't really a normal Foreseer thing either."

"Yeah, but you are…" He trails off as I give him a cold stare because he was about to say different, and I really dislike being called that. "Unique," he finishes, with a teasing smile that focuses all of my attention on his lips.

My heart sinks inside my chest, though, at the thought of kissing him. I'll never be able to kiss him again unless I figure out a way to get rid of the star's power, without killing myself or Alex.

"Gemma, I can tell there's something else bothering you," Alex says. "I can feel it..." His forehead creases as if the revelation has baffled him as well as me. "So please just tell me."

"You can feel it?"

He gives a one-shoulder shrug. "Sometimes when you're really upset... I know... but don't ask me how because I have no idea." He pauses. "But quit changing the subject and please for the love of God, tell me what's eating at you because it's starting to eat at me."

I grow quiet, trying to figure out how to explain that we can't be with each other anymore; at least not in a way that will cause us to develop feelings of love toward one another. That the Blood Promise we made to be together forever is meaningless.

"I have to tell you—" I finally work up the strength, but am interrupted by the sound of the front door slamming and then Aislin calling out, "Hello?!"

I instantly spring from the bed, searching the floor for my clothes, while Alex lazily gets to his feet as if nothing's wrong, as if we weren't just having hot, intense sex in probably the worst moment possible.

I get some jeans and a fresh t-shirt out of the dresser and start to get dressed.

"What's the rush?' Alex asks amusedly as he takes his time putting his jeans back on.

"Nothing." I tug the white shirt over my head in a hurry, then comb my fingers through my long brown hair in a lame attempt to tame the chaos of my tangled locks. "I just don't want her thinking that we're in here fooling around when we should be looking for Laylen."

There is a hint of annoyance in his eyes as he picks up a shirt that's on the floor and pulls it on. "But that's exactly what we were doing."

"I know but..." I trail off as Aislin calls out again and head out of the room, Alex slowly following behind me.

Aislin's in the living room, cheeks pink, her golden-brown hair is frizzy from the moisture of the spring air, and her shorts and t-shirt are stained with dirt as if she's been grave digging. I can tell immediately that something's up, something is upsetting her.

"What's wrong?" I ask as I straighten up my shirt.

Aislin shakes her head, pressing her lips together as if stifling a cry. "Laylen...Lay..." Suddenly she bursts into sobs, her head falling into her hands as she sinks onto the nearest chair.

I hurry over to her. "What happened to Laylen? And where's my mom?" I'm painfully reminded that reality that saving the world and staying away from Alex isn't my only responsibility. I also need to save a vampire who, at least from the last time I saw him, was dealing with blood thirst issues that I caused by begging him to bite me so he wouldn't die.

"Your mom's still out looking for him... I needed a break because I can't... can't..." Aislin cries harder, gasping for air. "I can't... do... this..."

I'm not spectacular with emotions, but I do my best and give her a pat on the back. "It's going to be okay. Just tell us what's wrong."

My attempt to soothe her is way better than Alex's. He rolls his eyes, appearing irritated. "Just spit it out, Aislin."

Looking hurt, Aislin wipes the tears away as she raises her head back up. "I can't find him anywhere... And I'm worried... what he might be doing."

"Me too," I agree, wanting to scream at myself for being so selfish just five minutes ago and only thinking about myself.

Alex drops down on the sofa across from us and props his foot on his knee. "Yeah, we all are, but freaking out isn't going to help us find him."

"You don't need to be rude," Aislin snaps. "I'm just a little upset, okay?" Tears well in her eyes again. "I never got to tell him I was... sorry... for everything." Tears pour out of her eyes and she abruptly shoves me back and takes off down the hallway, leaving me wide eyed and baffled, because honestly I thought only I reacted so dramatically.

"You know, sometimes I'm grateful I can shut off my emotions when I need to." Alex mutters. "It keeps me from doing things like that."

"Not all emotions are bad," I point out, sitting in the spot Aislin just evacuated.

"No they're not." Hunger burns in his eyes and emits in his voice, his breathing quickening uncontrollably as he looks at me. Then without notice, he's getting to his feet and crossing the room toward me, his arm extended as if he's going to grab me again and pull me into another irresistible kiss.

For a faltering second I stay motionless, wanting him to do it. But then I remember that I already had my selfish moment and it's time to fess up and deal with things the right way, so I lean back right as he's about to touch me.

His expression contorts with confusion as he withdraws his hand to his side and stops just in front of me. He assesses me intently and I wouldn't be surprised if he had a straight insight to my thoughts. "What are you not telling me?"

I take a deep breath and motion between us. "You and I can't—"

"What the fuck. You're head's bleeding." He cuts me off, squinting at my forehead.

"What?"

"There's blood all over the side of your head." He drops to his knees and his fingers brush my temple. This time I don't budge, letting him inspect, wondering what's going on.

Then my finger drifts to the area he's touching as I start to feel an aching sensation there and it is instantly coated with a warm, sticky substance. Blood. All over my hair and skin and now my fingers. I quickly jump to my feet and rush over to a mirror on the wall to examine my head. On the left side of my scalp, there is a deep cut covered by blood that trails down my cheek and is also matted in my hair.

"That wasn't there a minute ago." Alex moves up behind me to inspect the cut some more. "It was like it appeared out of nowhere."

"But then where did it come from." We exchange a puzzled look, but something in my mind is clicking. Why is the injury so familiar? And the pain spreading through my skull… I've felt it before. Suddenly it hits me, like a punch to the gut. "Oh my God."

Alex's arms protectively enclose around me. "What's wrong?"

"I think…" I don't finish and sprint across the living room for the back door.

"Where are you going?" Alex calls out, running after me.

I don't answer, throwing open the back door and leaping down the steps. Then I race across the sandy beach toward the cliff area where Nicholas knocked me out before handing me over to Stephan.

"Gemma!" Alex yells from at my heels. "Where the heck are you going?"

I push past a few people blocking the entrance chatting and drinking beers and they curse and flip me off. But I disregard them, calling over my shoulder to Alex, "I have to see something." I wind through the rocks, feel the bottom of my feet scrape open, but don't slow down. Blood continues to trickle out of the wound on my head and sweat beads my skin as the sun blazes down on me. Finally, I slow to a jog as I approach the mouth of the cliffs where the rocks part.

Alex halts beside me, wiping a bit of sweat from his forehead. "I get the whole need answers now thing, but fucking hell, will you please tell me what's going on?"

"I want to see if there's something back here..." I explain vaguely, wiping the sweat from my brow as I venture closer to the area Nicholas took me down at.

"Okay..." Alex walks beside me. "Could you be a little less vague?"

I scan the ground and rocks. "I'm looking for a sign that the past that was erased has taken place, if that makes any sense."

"Kind of." He squints against the sunlight as he searches the tops of the rocks. "But I thought you said that didn't happen." He shields his eyes with his hand. "That your father erased it, so why do you think there would be a sign?"

I look over my shoulder at him. "I thought he did but now..." I shake my head. "I have no idea what's going on, but if there's blood back here, then some-thing's up—something's not right, because the cut bleeding on my head right now was exactly where

Nicholas hit me before he kidnapped me and gave me over to Stephan." My head throbs and a warm line of blood drips down my skin. I press my hand against the wound and delve further into the cliffs cautiously, keeping an eye out for blood and a blond haired fae-rie.

When I arrive at the end of the path where rocks open up into a small sandy area, my heart rate accelerates. And my confusion multiplies.

Alex squeezes up to the side of me and squints down at the ground in front of our feet where a body lies in the sand. "What is that?"

"It's....me." I gaze down at myself, unconscious, laying in a pool of blood, wearing the clothes I had on when I'd been taken to the Wastelands. "Am I in a vision right now?" Out of the corner of my eye, I catch sight of a figure appearing and moving toward us. Nicholas. I jump back, knocking my shoulder into Alex's chest, and he steadies me with his hands.

Nicholas, who is usually alarmingly calm, appears as shocked as me. His golden eyes are wide, lips slightly parted, as he stares down at the *me* in the sand.

"How the hell did that happen..." He trails off as comprehension rises on his face and he looks up at me. "Wow, I'm *very* impressed." He starts clapping his hands mockingly, like the true asshole that he is.

"Bravo, I must say. You become more amazing each time our paths cross." He grins wickedly at me and then a split second later, he's lunging for me.

I don't have the reflexes of a cat by any means, and Nicholas is skilled in the art of lunging. Thankfully, Alex's reflexes are flawless and with one swift movement, he's positioned himself in front of me and clocks Nicholas in the jaw.

"Dammit..." Nicholas's eyes roll into the back of his head and he falls back, landing hard in the sand, out cold.

Alex shakes out his hand as he turns to me. "His head is as hard as a rock."

I laugh, but it swiftly vanishes as I step over Nicholas and make my way over to the body of *me* lying in the sand. Is it real? Or is she just a vision? Hesitantly I crouch down and place a hand on her arm. There's a zap that shoots through my body and jolts straight to my heart, more powerful than even the current of sparks between Alex and me. I gasp, feeling the past moment erase and evaporate into the wind, vanishing, as if it had never even existed at all.

As the body of me goes with it, my hand falls onto the sand. "Wow." I'm speechless as I stare at the empty spot. The ocean crashes against the other side of the rocks, birds sing in the distance, and the wind kisses my cheeks, the world becoming at peace with time, or at least that's what it feels like.

"Gemma." Alex puts a hand on my shoulder. "Are you okay?"

His hand falls from my shoulder as I rise to my feet. My mind is so wired from the power still lingering inside me that I can barely get my eyes to blink. "I think so, but I think I need to..." I clutch my head, where the wound was and note that it's no longer there. I should feel better, but I feel strangely dizzy and disoriented. "I think I need to lie down." I stagger to the side, my elbow slamming into one of the rocks. My skin scrapes open, Alex says something but his voice sounds far away as I collapse to the ground.

Chapter 5

Light everywhere. Encompassing me. Stealing the breath from my lungs. Stealing my heart. Alex and I by the lake, holding onto one another as if our lives depend on it. It will be okay. Ice. So cold. Death. Shadows emerging from the trees. I can't breathe…I'm dying…

My eyes shoot open and I gasp for air as I try to figure out where I am, what's real and what's an illusion.

"Breathe." Alex pats me softly on the back. "Just breathe. Deep breaths."

Inhale, exhale, inhale, exhale. Deep breaths. My breathing gradually returns to normal and my surroundings start to make sense again. The rocks. The warm sunlight spilling over me. The waves crashing against the shore nearby. Alex. His green eyes so full of worry.

"You know, I've worried more than I ever have since I met you," he says, attempting to make a joke as I sit up.

I force a smile, and then I try to get to my feet, bending my knees and pushing upward. But the world dances and I can't stay up, my legs instantly buckling and I fall to ground.

Alex kneels down in front of me, his hand finding my cheek, almost as if it's a magnet and my skin is metal. "You stopped breathing for a moment and I..." His gaze sweeps every inch of my body before residing back on my eyes. "I thought I'd lost you."

"Oh," is all I can think of to say.

I place my hand over his, the sensation of the deadly images I saw while I was out still crisp in my mind and haunting me to the point that I feel like I need comfort. "What do you think just happened? Not just with me stopping breathing, but with the vision thing."

"I have no idea." He nods his head at Nicholas still passed out on the ground behind us. "I wonder if he knows something, though."

"It looked like he might," I say, returning my attention back to Alex. "But even if he did, what are the odds he'll tell us the truth?"

Alex's green eyes sparkle mischievously in the sunlight. "Oh, there are ways to get him to tell us what we want to know." He gets to his feet and dusts the sand off his jeans. "They're just not very nice ways."

I feel a ping of pity for Nicholas. He has no control over what he does—the Mark of Malefiscus does. Although, he was annoying before he was branded. Still it doesn't mean he deserves to be hurt. Then again, I can't help but think of all the times he violated me, to the point where I'm pretty sure he was coming close to raping me.

"I'm so confused," I say, aloud not meaning to.

"About what?" Alex asks, circling around Nicholas with his hands on his hips.

I wish I could retract my statement because the last thing I want to do is talk to Alex about my feelings, but I find myself doing so anyway. "About why I feel the way I do."

He pauses, looking solely at me. "And how's that?"

I shrug, getting to my feet and leaning against the rock behind me. "I feel kind of bad for him."

Alex gapes at me. "You feel sorry for Nicholas?" He steps toward me, examining me closely. "Are you sure your head's okay?"

I nod, touching my head. "It's just that he's branded with the mark… and from what little I can remember, it has a lot of control over you."

"Yeah, but even when he's not possessed by the mark, he's an asshole."

"I know. I don't know what's wrong with me, but I just feel… well, bad for him." I scratch the back of my neck where the prickle is tickling. "I'm blaming it on the whole emotional thing. It confuses me some- times."

One side of his mouth lifts up to a half-smile. "I know." He steps toward me, reducing the rest of the space between us. "But trust me when I say that you never, ever have to feel sorry for him." His fingers tangle through my hair and before I can stop him, he pulls me in for a quick kiss, then moves away. "Now let's get him back to the house." He rubs his hands together, fully enjoying this. "I have big plans for him."

The prickle continues to dance on my neck, like little pointed shoes made of sharp metal. Poking. Pok- ing. Poking. Tormenting me. My emotions are in overdrive and I start to wonder if this is really about just feeling bad for Nicholas or if I'm feeling bad for Alex too because I'm keeping such a huge secret from him. But I can't help it. Every time I open my mouth, it seems as though another problem arises.

Dizziness overcomes me again. "I think I'm going to be…" I drop to the ground like a bag of bricks. The last thing I see is the sunlight before the sky above me darkens like nighttime only the stars are missing.

***

I wake up in the bed at the beach house, surrounded by curtains flapping in the light sea breeze. The door is open and I can hear voices coming from the living room. My head feels a lot clearer, although my body a little achy, but I still manage to easily sit up and swing my feet over the edge of the bed.

"Feeling better?" Alex's voice alarms me as he enters the room.

I stretch my arms out above my head and yawn. "Yeah, I think so. Although, I felt better the last time I passed out and still did it again about five minutes later."

He crosses the room to sit down on the bed, nervous energy gently flowing off him. "You're starting to worry me with all the times you've blacked out." He puts a hand on my forehead. "I'm worried that maybe... maybe I'm doing it somehow unintentionally."

"What do you mean? Why would you being doing it?" My walls start to go back up. It's not that I don't trust Alex, but at the same time our past has been full of lies and I can't help but be wary.

He puts his hand on my knee, his grip firm, subtly holding me in place. "I have to tell you something... about me." More tension builds and I calculate the distance to the door. "Relax," he says. "It's not something that's going to be life crushing, it's just something… well, something I don't tell a hell of a lot of people."

I meet his penetrating gaze. "Then why are you telling me?"

"Because I want you to trust me and trust comes from telling stuff I might not want to tell."

"Okay. I'm listening."

He takes a deep breath. "I have an ability that I haven't told you about yet." He pauses. "I can…" he withdraws his hand away from my leg to yank it through his brown hair, making it stick up in various directions, giving him that bedhead sexy look I love so much. "I can drain energy from people."

I think of the energy flowing around inside me right now, connected to him through the star. "When you say people, do you mean everyone or just me?"

"Everyone for the most part. I can make them tired when I need to, but with you, it works a little bit different. I literally drain the energy from you."

"Have you done it to me before?"

"Not that I know of or can remember," he says. "Although, from the details you told me about what happened when you tried to kill me and you were possessed, it sounded like I might have. And now I'm starting to wonder with all this passing out that you keep doing, if maybe I'm unintentionally doing it to you."

"I don't think that's what it is. What happened at the beach, at least the last time, felt like it came from my emotions. Sometimes it feels like they're too much to bare so my body just sort of shuts down." I could get angry that he didn't tell me about his ability earlier, but I'd be a hypocrite since I've been keeping something from him too.

Avoiding his gaze, I summon the strength to finally put the inevitable out there. "I need to tell you something." I force myself to meet his gaze. "About you and me... and it's bad.... Something your father told me while I was at the Wastelands." As soon as I mention his father, hatred mixed with vulnerability masks his face. "He told me that if you and I," I motion between us repeatedly, stalling. "If we... if we feel too much for each other... fall in love, then the star's power will eventually fade and die and you and I... you and I will fade away and die right along with it." Wow, that hurt more than I thought. A deep, tender ache begins to grow inside my chest, as if my heart is hollowing out.

He sits quietly for what feels like an eternity and I swear I actually can see when the lights go off in his eyes. "Well, okay then." He gets to his feet.

"That's all you have to say?" I follow after him as he strides out of the room, determined not to look at me. "After what I just told you."

He pauses, turning to face me, eyes cold as the day we first met. "What do you want me to say?" he asks. "We can't be near each other, so we won't."

"I never said we couldn't be near each other. Just that we couldn't feel..." The word was so hard to say, so foreign, never felt.

"Love," he finishes for me. "It's all the same." With that, he walks away and this time I let him, wondering if he meant that when he was around me, he does feel love.

Chapter 6

I let Alex be for the next few hours, figuring it's probably for the best. Let him be irritated with me. Still, it's hard being in the same room with him, knowing that all those intense, passionate, in-the-heat-of-the-moments were going to be no more.

"Is this really necessary?" I ask Alex the same question I've been asking him for a while. We're in the garage, the doors closed, the window blocked by a shelf so the only light is coming from the ceiling and the only way to see what's going on in here is by entering the garage, which is good, since if a neighbor or someone saw the scene in front of me, they'd more than likely call the cops.

Alex shrugs and then cracks his knuckles. "Maybe." It's hotter than hell in here, musty, stuffy. He has his shirt off, sweat dripping down his chest, his jeans riding low on his hips, giving me a full few of the muscles carving his midsection.

It's almost like he's taunting me, *ha ha this is what you can't have anymore.* So I try to stop staring at him and concentrate on what's going on, but I'm not sure it makes me feel any better. Despite my loathing for

Nicholas, seeing him tied up and being tortured is a bit difficult to watch. After Alex dragged him back to the house, he bound his hands with rope and then secured the rope to a beam that ran along the ceiling in the garage, pulling it tight enough that Nicholas is forced to stand on his tiptoes or hang from his arms. His lip is cut and bleeding, his skin is scraped on his side, and blood covers various parts of his body. His sandy blond hair is damp with sweat and his shoes fell off somewhere.

"Tell me what you know about what happened back on the beach," Alex demands as he paces in front of Nicholas.

Nicholas laughs but it's laced with pain. "Never."

Alex cranes his arms back and without warning, punches Nicholas in the stomach. "You better talk or it's going to get a hell of a lot worse."

Nicholas grunts, his back curved from the impact. He breathes in and out before speaking again, forcing a light tone. "You know, it's actually starting to tickle."

Alex clocks him again, this time in the ribs. I cringe at the cracking noise, like bones breaking. "I could do this all day," Alex tells Nicholas as he brings his arm up and slams his fist into Nicholas's jaw.

This continues for what feels like forever and I watch, wondering if I'm any better for doing nothing.

58

Just when I've come close to talking myself into leaving, the door opens up and Aislin enters. She has a handful of grapes and offers me some as if we're snacking and watching a movie.

Still, my belly is empty and I gratefully take some. "We should do something," I tell her, popping a grape into my mouth.

She looks at Alex as he takes another swing. "Like what? I hate to say it, but this needs to be done."

"Isn't there another way?" I ask, eating another grape. "Like maybe you could do a spell to get him to confess."

She finishes off the last of the grapes. "I can't."

"Why not?"

"Didn't Alex tell you? I lost my spell book."

"What? How?"

She shrugs, wiping her fingers on the sides of her jeans. "I'm not sure, but while you were passed out, I was sitting there looking through it and suddenly it disappeared. I have no idea what could have happened to it other than maybe another powerful witch did a Power of Possession spell and took it. Although what the hell they'd want with it is beyond me."

"Maybe it has a spell in there that theirs didn't."

"Maybe, but I doubt it," she says. "It was actually a pretty typical spell book, well at least from what I understand."

An image of a blond haired girl with blue eyes, wearing gloves and a wicked grin, holding Aislin's spell book pops into my head. The girl is with Laylen, talking to him like they're old friends, laughing as she tosses her hair from her shoulder. But as quickly as the image appears, it dissolves.

"Have you heard anything from Laylen by chance?" I massage the sides of my head with my fingertips. I think I might be exhausted and in need of some mental rest.

Aislin shakes her head, folding her arms over her chest. "Not yet."

"What about my mom?"

"No... Well, she checked in about an hour ago. Said she was in town and was going to keep looking."

"I worry about her being alone, especially since she just got out of The Underworld."

Aislin smiles sympathetically. "Don't worry. She's a Keeper and we're taught to recover quicker than most."

"Mentally recover?" I frown over at Alex with doubt. "Because it seems like he might be proving that theory wrong."

"That's just Alex." She pats my arm in a friendly manner. "And trust me, this is much better than how he used to be."

Alex continues to beat up Nicholas with no progress until finally I can't take it anymore. I march forward and snag Alex's arm before he can hit Nicholas again. His skin nearly scalds mine, mainly because the anger inside him is causing the sparks to crackle like fire. But I refuse to let him go and instead catch his eye. "Look, I know he's annoying and everything, but still... killing him isn't going to help us and beating him up isn't getting him to talk."

"Back off Gemma," Alex says through gritted teeth as he scowls down at my hand on his arm.

I free his arm. "No." I lean forward and whisper, "Look, I get that you're pissed off at me over what I told you, but take it out on me not him."

"You pity him." He's baffled. "Seriously?"

I shake my head. "No, I just hate watching all this pointless violence and I don't want you doing something that's going to make you hate yourself. Like kill him."

"I wouldn't hate myself if I did that," he assures me., wiping the sweat from his brow. "In fact, I'd be glad."

"Don't do that," I tell him, gently taking his hand. "Don't put up that tough guy douche bag façade again and go back to being a douche."

He stares at me intensely for a moment and I think I might be getting through to him, but then he's glaring at me and yanking his hand away. "Don't touch me."

It stings just a little, but I think I know enough to understand that he might just be hurting and this is his way of dealing with it. So I just stare at him, because arguing is pointless. The longer it goes on, the more stifling things get. The more the electricity coils in places it shouldn't. The more my fingers beg to touch him, rip the remaining clothes from his body.

Then Nicholas busts up laughing and shatters the moment. "Oh my God, look at you two. You both want to be together so badly, yet, if you do, you'll more than likely fall in love and kill each other. It's fucking hilarious."

Alex turns toward him, jaw set tight. "What did you just say?" His hands enfold into fists.

Nicholas gives him a bloody smirk. "I didn't say anything."

Alex takes a few threatening steps toward him, his boots scuffing the cement floor. "What do you know about Gemma and I killing one another if we fall in love?"

"Wait a minute?" Aislin rushes forward. "What do you mean you'll kill each other if you fall in love?" She puts her hands on her hips as she scowls at me then at Alex. "Why am I just hearing about this?"

"Because it doesn't matter at the moment." Alex waves her off, his gaze fixed on Nicholas. "Now start talking before I start beating the shit out of you again."

Nicholas shakes his head, his body swaying with the rope. Alex's skin reddens with rage as he elevates his fist. "God dammit. Why do you have to be such a pain in the ass?"

Nicholas writhes his body and attempts to wiggle his arms from the rope. But he's helpless and I think he knows it. Hell, there's so much blood on his face and clothes, it looks like he should be dead already. "Alright… I'll tell you." He pauses, his body still, relaxing. "But I want something in return." His gaze flicks in my direction.

Alex shakes his head as I tense. "No way."

"Then no deal," Nicholas says with a shrug, struggling to keep his toes on the floor.

"I don't think you're in much of a position to be making bargains." Alex lowers his arm to crack his knuckles. "Or do I need to remind you of that?"

"What do you want?" I step between them. "It doesn't hurt to hear what he wants."

"Gemma, be careful," Alex warns, but I shush him, putting my finger across his lips.

"Let's just hear him out and then make a decision, okay?" I say. His breath quickens simply from my touch. I'm starting to wonder just how powerful of a hold I have over him. Well, not me but the electricity. Biting my lip, I lower my finger, and then wait for Alex to say something, when he doesn't, I turn to Nicholas. "What do you want?"

The humor erases from Nicholas's face and he momentarily looks human, but I have to remember all the things he's done and the fact that he has the ability to manipulate my mind and make me see things that aren't real. "I want to stay here," he says.

"You want to what?" I gape at him. That wasn't what I was expecting at all.

"I want to stay here," he repeats as Alex shakes his head and Aislin makes this strangled, shocked noise. "After I tell you what I know, I want to be able to hang around here for a while."

"No way," Alex protests. "There's no chance in hell that'll ever happen."

"Yeah, I don't think that's such a good idea either." I point to the red and black triangular mark on Nicholas's forearm—the Mark of Malefiscus, pure evil. "Especially considering you have that on you and I know firsthand just how powerful that thing is."

"I know you do." His eyes twinkle with the knowledge that he might know all about the vision erased and what happened. It would make sense since he's a Foreseer and they can see practically everything. "And this mark is why I want to stay," Nicholas explains, trying to get his footing as sweat drips down his face to hips lips and jaw. "If Stephan can't find me, then he can't force me do things for him."

I look over at Alex. "Is that true?"

Alex shrugs. "I have no idea how the mark works, other than it's pure evil and the person who has it has to have evil in..." He trails off, recalling that in another time I had the mark.

"It's okay. I've already come to the conclusion that I have evil in my blood." I shrug, pretending it's no big deal. "And I think I know where it comes from now—from my father."

"You sure about that?" Nicholas questions with amusement.

"What do you know about it?" I wonder, suddenly seeing why Alex gets so frustrated with him.

He gives a shrug, but it looks awkward with his arms restrained above his head. "Let me loose and stay here and I'll tell you."

I tread with caution. "If we do that, then how do we know you're telling the truth and how can we trust you? You don't have a very good track record."

A grin expands across his face. "Guess you'll just have to take that risk."

Dammit. Why does the one person who seems to have the answers have to be a very obnoxious fae-rie/Foreseer that loves twisting things into riddles and making everything complicated?

I exchange a look with Alex and Aislin. "What do you guys think we should do?"

"I don't know...do you think we can trust him?" Aislin asked Alex with wariness.

He folds his arms across his chest, appearing annoyed and lost amongst many other things. "I have no fucking clue."

I glance down at the faint scar on my palm and get an idea. I extend my hand out in front of me, palm up. "I have an idea," I say then look at Nicholas. "Would you be willing to do a Blood Promise that you wouldn't do anything harmful to anyone and that you would tell us what we need to know in exchange for your freedom and staying here?"

Alex promptly starts protesting. "No fucking way," he says, at the same time Nicholas remarks, "Clever girl."

"Why not?" I ask Alex, lowering my hand to my side. "It's not like it's a bad thing to do or anything and it'll help us make sure this all works out the way that we want it to."

"Blood Promises can go wrong, Gemma." Alex frowns as he traces the scar on the palm of his hand. "The promise is unbreakable—you can't take it back. And if you say the wrong thing, you can end up making a promise you didn't intend to make."

"Is that what happened with us?" I ask, raising my brows in accusation. "Did you say the wrong thing? Or is it that you just want to take it back?"

He looks taken aback. "Why would you say that?"

I shrug indifferently. "Well, it'd make things easier right now for you, wouldn't it?"

He steps closer to me. "Even if we never made the promise, I'd still..." His tongue slips out of his mouth and wets his lips as he struggles for words. "I'd still fucking hate what's going on more than I've ever hated anything in my entire life." He takes another step toward me, so close the tips of our shoes brush against each other. "What I feel for you isn't based on some stupid star or promise or anything other than my emotions."

We're veering toward forbidden territory, about to jump off the cliff, at least he is. Even though I desperately want him to continue, I need to stop it before he does something he can't take back.

"Okay, we'll have to be really careful then when we make the blood promise." I change the subject. "You tell me exactly what to say."

He looks at me for a fleeting moment with hurt in his eyes before he shoves it all down and moves away from me. "Even with the Blood Promise, if my father shows up, Nicholas will more than likely still have to do what he asks since I'm pretty sure the Mark of Malefiscus is more powerful than a Blood Promise."

"Okay, well I guess we'll have to make sure your father doesn't find us then," I say. "I think it's worth the risk to get some answers, Alex."

Alex is unconvinced, but I already have made up my mind and turn to Nicholas. "Okay, you and I will make a Blood Promise. I'll promise you can stay here with us, and you'll promise that you'll answer all of my questions truthfully. And, you won't harm any of us while you're here, got it?"

Nicholas considers what I said then a grin slowly creeps up on his face. "I want one more thing."

"No way," I say firmly. "That's the deal. Take it or leave it."

He nods his head at Aislin. "I want Witch Girl over there to try and find a way to get this mark off my arm."

My head snaps in Aislin's direction. "Can you do that?"

Aislin ravels a strand of her hair around her finger. "I don't know...I mean, there might be a spell that could remove a mark, but I've never heard of it, or I might not be powerful enough to actually pull it off. Plus, my spell book is gone so it makes finding the spell to do it even more complicated."

"You know other witches, don't you?" Nicholas says in a condescending tone. "Talk to them—see if they know how."

"Maybe I could see if someone knows a spell that would work," Aislin says. "But it's going to take time and a lot of searching probably, in places I don't generally go."

"We're talking black magic?" Nicholas asks.

"More or less," Aislin replies and Nicholas seems twistedly pleased by this.

"Good, then we have a deal." He smirks at all three of us.

I glance at Alex who's shaking his head, arms folded, muscles taut, but he doesn't utter a word. "Okay, we have a deal," I say, wondering when I became the spokesperson of the group. I stick my hand in Alex's direction. "Do you have a knife on you? So I can cut my hand and make the promise."

Still frustrated, he stuffs his hand into the pocket of his jeans and retrieves a small, silver knife. "I still don't think this is a good idea."

I take the knife from him and flip open the blade. I try to keep a steady hand as I aim the knife at my palm. "So I just cut and then what?"

Alex sighs, finally giving up on being stubborn, then takes the knife from me, and then holds my hand in his. He draws a line across the scar on my palm with his thumb before releasing my hand. "I need your other hand to do it."

I give him my other hand like he asks. "Can we not do the promise in the same place twice or something?"

His head is angled down so I can't see his expression. "No, you can do that, but I don't want to do it on the scar that was from *our* promise—that's mine."

It might be the sweetest thing he has ever said to me. I bite back a smile, though, because it's a feeling that's bitterly sweet.

"Man, you two are going to kill each other quickly, aren't you?" Nicholas reminds me of what I can't have.

Alex shoots him a glare as he touches the cold blade to my skin. "I'm going to cut your hand and his," he tells me. "Then you'll press your palm to his and repeat exactly what I say, alright?"

I nervously nod. "Alright."

"And be very careful that you repeat *exactly* what I say," he stresses.

"Don't you need to untie Nicholas first?" I ask.

"I'm not going to let him go until the promise is made," Alex states firmly. "You'll just have to reach up to his hand." Then very vigilantly he makes a small cut along my palm. Blood seeps out of the wound and I quickly cup my hand. Then Alex moves over to Nicholas, reaches up over his head, and with less carefulness, slices Nicholas's hand open. Blood drips out of the wound and down his bare arm.

Stepping back, Alex closes the blade then tosses the knife onto the floor. "Okay, put your hand up to his," he says to me.

Gathering up the courage, I step forward and get on my tiptoes to press my bleeding palm against Nicholas's. The smell of flowers and rain is overwhelming and his nearness makes me uncomfortable as he leans over and smells my hair.

"We should have done this a long time ago." He breathes in my scent. "God, you smell so divine."

I slant my head away from him. "Back the hell off, faerie boy or I'll drop kick you in the balls."

Aislin snorts a laugh as Nicholas chuckles lowly in my ear. "Sounds kinky to me," he says.

I roll my eyes. "Only in your dreams."

"Repeat *exactly* what I say, Gemma," Alex says, interrupting us. *"EGO votum permissum."*

I speak slowly to avoid mistakes. *"EGO... votum...permissum."*

"Vos subsisto hic quod Andron."

"Vos... subsisto... hic quod... Andron." My voice shakes.

"Mos capto aufero vestri vestigium."

"Mos capto... aufero... vestri... vestigium."

Alex and I release a breath of relief, then Alex points a finger at Nicholas. "You better repeat exactly what I say. No changing or adding anything, understand? Or I'll kill you." He says it with a straight face and I have no doubt that he just might do it.

After Nicholas agrees, Alex tells him what to say, speaking the words carefully. Nicholas repeats everything correctly. But I have no idea what's being said, so I'm putting a lot of trust in Alex. I analyze the idea of how much I'm trusting him at the moment and come to the conclusion that perhaps my feelings toward him might be drifting into the unsafe zone. But I haven't felt the prickle yet nor have I felt anything that's stopped and made me think, *hey, that's got to be love.*

After the Blood Promise is made, Alex cuts the rope and frees Nicholas. He falls to the floor on his knees and rubs his wrists as he wipes the blood from his lip with the bottom of his t-shirt. "God, that feels good."

"Now tell us everything you know about my father. Gemma. The Vision. No holding back." Alex bends down and collects the knife from the floor.

"Can we at least sit down?" Nicholas asks, sounding pained.

Alex shakes his head as he cleans the blood off from the knife on the side of his jeans. "Whatever, let's just get this over with."

Chapter 7

In the living room, Alex sits down on the sofa next to Nicholas, not wanting me near either himself or the faerie—I'm still trying to figure out which one. I take a seat on the couch across from them beside Aislin. The curtains are drawn so there's minimal sunlight and heat flowing in through the windows, but the tension makes the air stifling.

Alex puts his knife on the table, kicks his feet up, and sits back. "Alright, start talking."

"About what?" Nicholas presses back a grin and sinks back in the chair, having to move slowly from the pain Alex inflicted while beating him up. "I can't seem to remember what any of this was about."

Afraid Alex might snap, I chime in. "How about you tell us what happened on the beach," I suggest. "Why there was another me there? I erased a vision, right?"

"Yes." His eyes pierce into me and make me squirm. "But it would also be an example of how extraordinary you are."

Let the running around in circles begin. "Define why that makes me extraordinary."

Nicholas flexes his mangled hand, wincing from the pain. "Because you erased a vision, which is something that's completely forbidden and could have severe consequences. Plus, not a lot Foreseers can do that." His eyes darken as they elevate to me. "If I wanted to, I could turn you into the Foreseers… you know there's punishment for erasing visions. Or we could do it the easy way and you and I could go into one of the bedrooms and I could punish you myself, just so you won't ever be a naughty girl again."

I crinkle my nose as Aislin makes an ewe face and Alex starts to close in on him. "What kind of a punishment?" I hurry and say, trying to keep the conversation moving forward. I can't help but think of my father and the strange place he's in. Is that the punishment?

Nicholas grins. "Well, it would require you naked and lots of whips and ropes."

"Not that punishment." I roll my eyes, making a repulsed face. "I mean, punishment from the Foreseers."

"I don't know for sure." Nicholas muses over something, tapping his finger on his swollen lips. "I've only heard of one Foreseer being punished for erasing a vision before."

"Do you know who he is? And where he is?" I'm trying to be as vague as possible but still get the answers that I want.

Nicholas shakes his head. "Our kind don't like to talk about things like that because...well, I think, because it reminds everyone of how much control and power Foreseers really have over everything."

I wonder if he realizes how right he is. Look at what my father did. *He* changed the entire course of the world and not in a positive way.

I get up and grab the crystal ball from the end table. "So can you explain to me what this is?" I ask, turning and holding up the crystal ball.

"Where the hell did you get that?" The glow of the crystal reflects in Nicholas's greedy eyes as I set the ball down on the coffee table and sit back down.

"That's not important." I hope I'm not making a mistake by showing it to him. "What's important is that you tell me what it is and how I can use it."

Nicholas's hand drifts for the crystal ball, hesitating, before he picks it up. Alex stiffens and so do I. I don't know what the crystal ball does. For all I know, it may have enough power to destroy us. That kind of an object shouldn't be in the hands of someone like Nicholas.

He gazes at the crystal ball in awe. "This is what we Foreseers refer to as a mapping ball. They're very rare." He turns over the crystal in his hand. "In fact, they're pretty much nonexistent." He bites his lip as he sets the ball down on his lap. "They hold a map of someone's life and show all the decisions they've made... although, some mapping balls are used to keep a secret hidden in the midst of thousands of their memories. It really is the most amazing thing." His withering gaze makes me shy back in the seat. "So whose is it?"

I glance at Alex, wondering if I should divulge that information to Nicholas. Alex presses me with a stern look, warning me to keep quiet.

"There's no use trying to keep it from me," Nicholas says. "Because I'm sure you're going to want to know how to use it, and that means you and I are going to have to go inside it."

"Inside it?" I ask, dumbfounded and Nicholas simply nods. Great. The last thing I want to do is go wandering around in my father's memories with the perverted faerie. But I don't really have a choice. "It's my father's," I tell him.

"I thought you told me you didn't know who your father is?" Nicholas questions.

"I just recently discovered who he was," I explain with an evasive shrug. "A lot of shit's happened since the last time we talked, well at least in this version of our lives."

"Yes, it has," Nicholas agrees, glancing down at the mark on his arm, and then returning his attention to me. "How did you find out who your father was? And how did you get a hold of his mapping ball?"

"My mom gave it to me," I lie with a shrug.

He rests his arms behind his head and puts his bare feet up on the table. "You managed to save her from The Underworld, then? Wow, again I'm impressed with your breathtaking ability." He winks at me. "And beauty."

"Yeah, and without your help I might add." I glare at him.

"I wouldn't say that." A grin creeps across his face. "Since I gave you the Ira."

"After you kidnapped me and chained me to the wall," I retort. "Don't give yourself credit where credit isn't earned. All you do is trick people and make things all messy and overly complicated."

He bites at his bottom lip with desire in his eyes. "You're getting awfully wound up right now. I like it."

"Fuck you."

"That's what I'm trying to do."

I about jump up from the seat to strangle him, but Aislin stops me, sticking her arm out in front of me like a barricade.

"Don't let him get to you," she says. "He likes it more than he hates it."

She's right. Nicholas does seem to get his kicks from pissing me off, so I sit back down and try to relax. "What's the purpose of the mapping ball?" I ask as calmly as I can.

Nicholas rolls his eyes. "I already told you it's to keep track of the things someone has done in their lifetime. If that is your dad's, then when we go inside it, we should be able to follow a map of his life."

Alex's forehead creases. "Why would your dad give this to you?" he asks me. "What does he want you to see?"

"I thought you said your mom gave it to you." Nicholas slants forward with a look of intrigue on his face. "Did you just get caught in a lie?" he asks me.

I give Alex a *really* look, wondering what's wrong with him. It's not like him to be so careless. "My dad said it would tell me how to save the world from Stephan, or at least fix the world's future… And if it holds a map of his life, then maybe I can see what vision he erased and recreated to make it so Stephan could end the world."

Nicholas claps his hands. "Bravo. You figured that one out all on your own."

"You're such and asshole," I snap. "You could have just told me that to begin with."

"I know a lot of things I choose not to share with you," he replies. "It's what makes life fun."

"But you have to tell the truth—you made the Blood Promise," I say, questioning if something went wrong.

"They're called loopholes, Gemma," Nicholas says with a satisfied look. "You have to ask me the question in order for me to tell you what I know. I don't just have to give you all my secrets."

"Okay, so do you know how to fix all of this then?" I ask. "Do you know what I need to do to save the world—to put everything back to the way it was like my father told me to do?"

Nicholas smiles, sitting lazily back in the chair. "I do. Would you like me to tell you?"

Fucking faeries. "Yes, Nicholas.' I force tolerance as Alex gives me an *I told you so look*, like I should now understand why he gets so aggravated with him, which I do. "I'm asking you to please share everything you know about mapping balls and Stephan's evil plan to end the world."

81

Aislin's phone starts ringing from inside her pocket. She takes it out and when she looks at the screen, she mutters, "Whose number is that?" She gets to her feet and heads out of the room as she answers it.

I redirect my attention back to Nicholas. "Start talking."

He does some weird bow thing as if he's obeying my command. "What would you like to know, princess?"

I press back my aggravation. "How to fix the vision back to what it was."

Nicholas scoops the mapping ball up in his hand, gets up, and wanders around the coffee table toward me. Alex begins to get to his feet but I shake my head at him.

"The thing about visions," Nicholas plops down on the sofa next to me and rotates the crystal ball in his hand, "is that everything is connected to each other."

"I'm not sure what you mean or how that'll help me fix the vision." I scoot away from him.

Nicholas stares down at the mapping ball, glimmering in the light. "In the Foreseer world, every vision is connected so say you make the decision to become a singer. You go down to the local talent show, try out, win, and go on become a famous singer." His fingers fold tightly around the crystal ball.

82

"Each one of those events that took place in your life to get you to the grand finale would be seen as their own vision. The decision, the trying out, the winning— all of them led to you becoming famous. They're all connected to one another—each one had to happen in order for the other one to happen."

"So if I never made the decision to become a singer," I say. "Then none of the rest would have happened—I would have never tried out or went on to make a career in singing."

"Exactly," Nicholas says with a snap of his finger. "And if a Foreseer wants to change the path of your life, he could just alter the first event and it could change everything from that point on. So say he put the idea in your head to become a ballerina. But on your way to tryouts, you left a minute later because you had to put on your tutu so you get in a car accident and die."

"But how could changing what I wanted to be, change my life that much?" I ask. "How can one tiny thing fuck up everything so that I'd die?"

"Haven't you ever heard of the butterfly effect?" he asks, arching his brows.

"Yeah, I learned about it in one of my classes." Classes. Such a normal thing to say yet it feels so abnormal.

"Well, it's like that. Change one small thing in your life and it alters everything. Ruin it or sometimes make it better, depending on what you do." He pauses, mulling something over with a thoughtful expres-expression. "I'm not sure what your father erased and recreated in order to get the world to end, but for us to stop it without doing too much damage, the best thing to do is to erase him before he changes the event. Well, not actually erase your father, but we would go into the mapping ball, find the memory of your father where he changed the vision, and erase him before he does it... like you did with yourself on the beach."

"And how are we supposed to find the exact memory?" I remove the crystal ball from Nicholas's hand. "If this thing is full of them."

Nicholas taps the side of his head. "That answer is in here. Literally."

My mood plummets. "In your head? You have got to be kidding me."

"Actually I am." He winks at me and positions his finger to the side of my head, disregarding the dirty look I give him. "It's actually in yours, which makes more sense if you think about it."

"My dad said the same thing to me," I say. "But I'm still lost."

"I'll explain more when we get in there," he says, lowering his hand to his lap. "It more easy to *show* you then to explain it you."

I sigh wearily as I recline back against the armrest. "And what if the vision my father changed still ends up leading to death?" I look over at Alex, thinking about the vision I saw right before I was dropped into the place where my father was. Alex and I by the lake, dying in each other's arms.

"It doesn't matter. It's how things were—are supposed to be." Nicholas traces the Foreseers' mark on his wrist, an *S* outlined by a circle. "Despite how powerful some of us get, Foreseers are only supposed to *see* visions, not change them or control them to our liking. No one should ever have that much control."

For a second, Nicholas actually seems like a decent person who cares about the world and has values. It's strange seeing him like this, serious and somewhat normal.

My father seems like the opposite. He changed a vision so the world would end in the most horrible way. Everything's going to freeze and all the witches, fey, vampires, and Death Walkers linked to Maleficus are going to run the streets killing everyone.

"Let's go then." I sit up straight. "I want to get this over with as quick as possible. The sooner we put everything back together, the sooner we can maybe all have a normal life." I can't help but glance at Alex. Is there hope for us yet?

"That's easier said than done." Nicholas snatches the mapping ball away from me. "This thing uses a lot of power. It's not as simple as placing your hand on it and going into it, like the other crystal balls you've used in the past." He throws the ball in the air and catches it, making me tense. "We need the power of the main crystal ball that all the other crystal balls run off in order to pull this off."

"The giant crystal ball that sucks its energy away from people?" I shudder at the memory of Alex strapped to the crystal with tubes embedded into his skin, along with a ton of other people.

"That would be the one," Nicholas says uncaringly.

"And the Foreseers are going to just let us take the power?" I ask doubtfully.

Nicholas looks down at his hand as he opens and closes it. "No, we steal the power and bring it back with us and use it here. It's safer that way."

"You actually think I'm going to let you go off to the City of Crystal alone with her." Alex gets up and walks over to us, sitting on the armrest just behind me.

"You could always let me go by myself and hope I'll come back," Nicholas replies snidely. "But I'm guessing you're not a fan of that idea either."

"Alex, back off. I can handle this," I say, not meaning to sound so rude, but it kind of slips out in my tone. "You have got to stop trying to protect me all the damn time."

"How am I supposed to stop doing something, when it's all I want to do?" He brushes his fingers across the back of my neck. "All I want to do is protect you. That's it. I can't even think clearly when I know you're in harm."

Recollection clicks in my head. He said that once to me, in another time, in the erased vision, before I ran off and got captured by Nicholas. It's strange that I'm remembering these little details, instead of them fading like the event did.

"Yeah, I give you two a day before you end up killing one another," Nicholas remarks with a laugh. "Seriously, it's like watching mild porn, watching you two eye fuck each other every two seconds."

"We'll be fine." Although, I'm not sure I believe my own words. *Fine*. Nothing feels fine. Not me. Not Alex touching me. Because he shouldn't be just touching me. He should be holding me. Kissing me. Slipping inside me over and over again...

"We have a problem," Aislin announces as she whisks into the room, interrupting my dirty thoughts. "A big problem."

"Of course we do," Alex says with an eye roll his fingers coming to rest on my back. "The world is going to end unless we fix it."

She shakes her head and puts her hands on her hips. "No, not that problem." Her eyes land on me. "Gemma, your mom just called and told me that she found Laylen and that he's in trouble."

"What kind of trouble?" The pitch of my voice is alarmingly high and I reach out to grip something for support and end up grabbing Alex's knee. "He didn't... bite someone did he?"

"He's..." She trails off, giving a cautious glance at Nicholas before leaning in and lowering her voice. "Maybe we should discuss this in private."

"Why? He can't go anywhere," I point out, but she is still hesitant.

"Just say whatever it is," Alex says, his finger tracing circles on my back. I wonder if he's even aware that he's touching me like that.

"He's at..." She lowers her voice even more and positions herself so her back is to Nicholas. "He was at the Red Dragon."

"Please don't tell me that's another club," I grimace, slumping against Alex. "I really don't want to do anymore clubs as long as I live, at least not ones with poisonous drinks."

"Oh, it's a club," Alex says dryly. "An exclusive club for anyone and anything that has a thirst for the evil side—much worse than the Black Dungeon."

"God, this is all my fault," I say, frustrated with myself.

"This isn't your fault," Alex assures me. "It's Laylen's. What he does is his choice."

I abruptly feel like I'm being strangled, invisible fingers winding around my neck. "Wait. If there's vampires at this club, they might kill him because he killed Vladislav." Panic overcomes me, makes the room spin as my lungs shrink.

"Oh my God! Would you two shut up!" Aislin yells, practically spitting in our faces as she stomps her foot. "I said he was at the Red Dragon, but someone we know picked him up from there and now he's safe, well more or less."

"Who picked him up?" I ask at the same time Alex says, "Fuck. Just what we need. I really don't want to deal with her shit right now."

I look over my shoulder at him and give him a funny look. "You know this person?"

Alex fidgets uncomfortably. "Yeah, more or less," he says in a tight voice with regret in his eyes.

"I know she lives close by here and everything." Aislin looks about as hurt as a wounded animal. "But I just never thought Laylen would contact her over me... us."

"Would someone please explain who *her* is?" I ask in the nicest tone I can summon.

Aislin waits for Alex to explain but he avoids her gaze and she sighs. "It's Stasha. She used to be a Keeper—well, I guess she technically still is, but she...decided she didn't want to be part of the circle anymore because of him." She nods her head at Alex who looks like he wants to be anywhere but here.

"Why would she leave because of him..." I stop talking, starting to put two and two together.

Nicholas stands up from the couch and leans in my face. "Because she and Alex used to be *lovers*, but since he's emotionally dead inside, he broke her heart." He pouts out his bottom lip, still puffy from when Alex clocked him.

I almost slap him, even though he's just telling me the truth. But the truth hurts in a way I had never felt before. I mean, I knew Alex dated and had girlfriends and everything, but I don't know. Talking about it is emotionally agonizing, raw and painful, like open wounds.

I clear my throat several times before I speak again. "So what do we do next? Call Laylen? Or do we just need to go get him? And is this Stasha girl keeping an eye on him because he needs to be watched, just in case." I sound like his mother. Jesus.

"Your mom didn't say anything about that." Aislin frowns. "She just said she found him standing outside the Red Dragon talking to Stasha, and when she went to go get him, he took off with her."

"My mom's headed back here, right?" I ask as I push Nicholas out of my way so I can get to my feet. "Now that she's found him."

Aislin gives a fleeting panicked look at Alex then back at me. "Yeah, I think she is."

Something's wrong. I make my way around the sofa so I'm standing in front of her. "You're keeping something from me, about my mother."

Aislin swiftly shakes her head. "No, she's headed back here now—I'm sure of it. So just relax. Besides, we really need to go get Laylen now since Stasha probably isn't the best person for him to be around."

A ripple of concern courses through me. "Why not?"

"Stasha can be a little on the...unsympathetic side," Alex says. "And that's probably the last thing Laylen needs right now."

"I still can't believe halfy finally went off the deep end." Nicholas laughs sardonically. "I always thought he was a little crazy."

"He didn't go off the deep end!" I shout, completely losing control over my emotions. I feel insane, the prickle poking and stabbing and eating away at the back of my neck as I shove Nicholas backward, causing him to slam against the coffee table. "It's my fault he wants to drink blood. Not his. I made him drink mine because I selfishly couldn't face the emotion of death."

It grows so quiet I swear I could hear a pin drop. I realize why moments later. They pity me. All of them.

"I don't want your pity," I say, hurrying for the front door. "I just want to go get Laylen and fix this mess."

"I'll get the car keys." Aislin backs for the kitchen. "It's not too far of a drive from here and I don't want to risk transporting too many people."

After she leaves, Nicholas leans against the wall, eyes on Alex as he grabs his shirt from the back of the chair and tugs it on. "You should probably warn her of what she can do."

Alex narrows his eyes at him, but when I look at him for an explanation, he sighs. "You remember when I told you that some Keepers have gifts, like Sophia's gift of…" He looks guilty for bringing up my soul detachment and quickly works his way around it. "And what I told you I could do?" he asks and I nod. "Well, Stasha has a gift too." He rubs the back of his neck tensely as he walks over to me. "She possesses the gift of death."

"She can kill me?" I shiver.

"Not for fun," Alex clarifies. "She just can kill, you know, kill if she wants to by touching someone."

"So she can kill me if she touches me?" I ask, my eyes widening as images strike my head of the blonde girl gripping at my throat.

"Only if she wants to," he says, ruffling his hair into place.

"Well, that sounds lovely," I say sarcastically. "And I have this feeling that she might want to."

"I won't let her hurt you," Alex promises, grazing his finger down my cheekbone, but then swiftly pulls away.

"We should get going." Aislin says as she returns the room, tossing Alex the car keys. "Stasha didn't answer her phone, so we're going to have to just show up there unannounced."

I aim a finger at Nicholas. "What are we going to do with him?"

Alex rubs his jawline, deliberating. "We could tie him back up in the garage and let him hang there until we get back."

"Or tie him to the rack on the roof like skis," I joke and Alex smiles, chuckling under his breath while Nicholas glowers at me.

"I think we should take him," Aislin says. "If someone shows up here while we're gone, he'll tell them everything—you know he will."

We all agree that's probably the best way, then we hide the mapping ball in a safe place and leave the house. Minutes later, we're driving down the highway, toward the next town where Stasha lives. The land is blanketed by night, the moon shining amongst the silver stars, and the ocean sings a lullaby as it sweeps against the shore.

The inside of the car is hot, due to the humid air and the electricity. Alex is driving and I'm in the backseat next to Nicholas, who is practically like an air freshener with his rainy, floral scent. It's too much and, finally, I roll down the window and breathe in the fresh air.

"You doing okay back there?" Alex asks, glancing at me in the rearview mirror.

I fan my hand in front of my face. "Yeah, it's just a little hot back here."

Nicholas lets out a loud snore as he wiggles in the seat, trying to rest his head on my shoulder, but I push him in the other direction. He dozed off the minute we pulled out of the driveway and Aislin passed out not too shortly after.

"It *is* hot in here," Alex agrees, giving me a tired smile. "But I think it's usually that way when you and I are in a confined space together." He rolls down his window too, letting more ocean air ventilate the car.

"Magic" by *Coldplay* hums through the speakers, a soft beat that's making me want to go to sleep too.

"Are you tired?" Alex glances at the time on the dashboard. "You can take about a fifteen minute nap if you want to."

I yawn. "Yeah, a little, but I'll stay awake."

"You should get some rest," he insists. "You need to be awake when we get there just in case something happens."

Suddenly, I'm wide-awake and I scoot forward in the seat and rest my arms on the center console. "You act like Stasha is going to murder me the moment I walk in the door."

"No, she's not *that* bad, but..." He pauses, wavering. "But she has some jealousy issues, which got worse when we broke up."

I can't help but wonder if we're broken up, Alex and I, or if we were technically even together. "Did you love her?"

His head whips in my direction. "Did I love Stasha?" he asks, almost in horror.

I nod. "I'm just wondering... if you've ever felt... that." I can't help but think of when we were in The Underworld and he said it to me. I had wondered if he meant it—still do. Part of me wants him to but the other doesn't because it'd put us half way to the end of *us*—all I would do is need to reciprocate.

He carries my gaze as he holds onto the steering wheel, annunciating each word when he says, "No, I never loved Stasha or anyone else I've been with." Again, I wonder if this includes me. "That's why I dated her...It was easy not to feel things with her...unlike with some people." He looks back at the road as my skin starts to tingle.

Stop thinking about him like that. Just stop. Find something else to talk about. "Have you ever been happy before?"

He relaxes. "Once or twice. You?"

"Maybe." I cross my arms on the console and slant forward to get a better look at his face. "What about scared? Because I feel that one all the time, although I'm doubting you ever do."

He brings his lower lip in between his teeth. "No, I have… When I first met you I was scared shitless and every time something happens to you, every time you get hurt or pass out, it scares me."

Again, we're heading in the no go zone, like two stars gravitating toward each other. "What other things have you felt?" I ask, knowing I shouldn't.

He seems reluctant to answer, but does anyway. "Anger. Frustration. Pain. Sadness." He pauses, looking at me instead of the road yet still managing to keep the car perfectly aligned in the lane. "Desire. What about you?"

"What other emotions have I felt?"

He shakes his head slowly, brings his hand away from the steering wheel, and puts his finger on my throat and draws a line down to my chest where he can probably feel my heart beating rapidly. "Have you ever felt desire?"

I can barely breathe. This wasn't my intention. In fact, I was trying to do the opposite, yet once again we can't stop touching each other and "eye fucking" as Nicholas put it.

"I feel it now," I say, boldness slipping out of me in a way it never has.

He groans, eyes flaring with desire. "Fuck, Gemma, I—"

"Alex stop!" I scream as a shadowy figure runs out in the road. Alex slams on the breaks as his arm shoots out in front of me, securing me in place. Tires screech. The car lurches forward...metal crunches...a bright light...yellow eyes... blackness...

Then nothing but quiet.

Chapter 8

I have never felt pain like this before. It's as if my body has compressed into a small, warped ball, my bones broken and bending in ways that shouldn't be possible. Everything hurts so badly. Death. I have to be dead.

"Gemma," someone says, but their voice sounds so far away. "Gemma, can you hear me?"

Wait a minute. I know that voice. It's the most wonderful voice in the world. I lift my eyelids, even though it's excruciatingly painful, and see the beautiful guy staring down at me with the brightest green eyes I'd ever seen.

"Are you alright?" the guy asks, leaning over me, looking so worried. All I want to do is hug him. Hug in the midst of the stars which seem to be dancing around me, so pretty.

I turn my head to nod, but it doesn't budge. There's gravel in my hair and stuck to my skin, along with something warm and liquid.

A girl joins the guy. I know her too. She has tears in her eyes and dirt and blood in her golden brown hair and she looks terrified.

"Look." She points at my stomach. "Alex, I don't think…"

The guy's eyes widen and with one swift movement, he scoops me up in his arms. "Get us out of here," the guy shouts at the girl as he cradles me against his chest, making me feel safe. "Now!"

She gapes at him helplessly. "Where do you want me to take us?"

"To Stasha's." There's panic on the guy's face, and I want to tell him it'll be okay—everything will be okay—but I can't seem to find my voice. "You have your crystal, right?" he asks the girl.

"Yeah, but what about him?" She turns and points at something on the ground near a pile of twisted metal that's on fire, smoke rising to the sky.

"We'll have to leave him here," he says. "If we don't get her out of here, she might not make it. Besides, you know they take care of their own when it comes to this sort of thing."

"Yeah, I know." The girl is disheartened, tears streaming down her cheeks. "Let's go then."

The boy says something else to me, but I can only see his lips moving. My eyelids are so heavy, so I shut them.

***

100

I'm dying. There is no pain, no anguish, no burden of the star. Everything feels complete, except for one thing. A piece of me is missing. Not an actual piece, but something I was connected to—electrically connected to. Alex. I need Alex. I feel so empty without him, but what does that mean? Does the fact that he seems to make me feel whole mean that I'm in love with him.

Love.

Forbidden.

I try to open my eyelids and see where I am, measure what I need to do to escape this hollowing feeling burrowing on the inside of me, but I can't, so I start to surrender, give up, let it gnaw the rest of me apart until I won't be anything but a shell. And for a brief instant, I feel better because I don't feel a thing.

"You can't give up Gemma," my father whispers. "You need to fix my mistakes."

"But I can't move," I tell him. "Everything hurts. My body… life… it's too hard."

"I know," he replies. "Trust me, I know how hard things can seem and how it seems like everything is up against you, but it'll get better. You just have to fight until you get there."

"But what if I can't?" I ask. "What if I'm not a fighter?"

"But you are… You got this far, didn't you? Now
open your eyes," he says. "Today isn't the day you're
going to die. Now fight for that."

Fight. *My eyelids slowly lift open. Light hits my
pupils, engulfs me. I can see the future again. Alex
and I by the lake. Hugging each other to our death as
a wall of ice surrounds us. I feel as though I should be
freezing to death, but there's so much warmth radiat-
ing between us that it spills around the world.*

***

I awaken peacefully, opening my eyes as if I've
woken up from a serene nights rest. But seconds later, the pain rises in my body and I let out a moan as I
take in where I am. In an unfamiliar bed, covered with
a blanket and the room is crammed with plants. They
are everywhere. On the shelves, the dresser and
leafy vines dangle from the ceiling.

I slowly sit up, hunching over as my stomach
burns in protest. I lift the bottom of my t-shirt and see
a very large section of my stomach is bandaged up. I
sift through my memories, trying to recollect how I got
here, hurt, but I'm drawing a blank.

"We got in a car accident," Alex says and I turn
my head toward the doorway. He's standing there

with his arms crossed, bags under his eyes and his hair sticking up, shirt and jeans torn and stained with blood.

"You look tired," I say. "Are you okay?"

"Am *I* okay? Gemma, you should only be worried about if you're okay right now."

"Where are we?" I ask, pulling the bottom of my shirt back over my stomach as I gaze around at all the plants.

He sits down on the foot of the bed, leaving some distance between us. "At Stasha's. The plants are healthy for her gift."

Pieces of what happened are starting to come back to me, but I don't think in order because they make no sense. "We were in a car accident... I can barely remember leaving the house."

His gaze flicks to my head, like he's checking for injuries he might have missed. "A Death Walker ran out into the road," he explains. "We hit it and ended up crashing the car."

"What about the Death Walker?" I ask. "Did it die?"

He gives me a look. "It can't die, only from the Sword of Immortality."

"So it's still alive?" I ask anxiously.

He reluctantly nods. "Thankfully, though, it was just one... and it ran off after we hit it... although I'm not sure what it was doing there in the first place and alone."

"Do you think it caused the accident on purpose? That maybe your dad sent it?"

"I'm not sure why he'd just send one." He leans back against the footboard with a quizzical look on his face. "And what I really don't get is why he's not coming here himself to get us."

Something clicks, another lost memory of an erased time. "While I was in the Wastelands, Stephan said something about when you reflected the *memoria extracto* or whatever the memory erasing rock was called, that it did something and he had to keep his distance for a while."

This makes Alex even more lost. "Why, though?"

"Maybe because of the *sacrificium protegat*." I say it robotically, not even sure what the words mean.

"Where did you learn about that?" Alex asks curiously.

"I have no idea..." A voice whispers to me inside my head, one I've heard before but can't place from where. Not because I've forgotten, but there seems to be some sort of wall blocking me from putting it together. "It just popped into my head."

He ponders this, looking concerned. "Just a second." Without explaining, he wanders out of the room, leaving the door open behind him. Voices drift from somewhere and after a bit, I get to my feet to go see what's going on. But I stop as I remember who Stasha is and what she can do. It's not that I'm afraid of her, well maybe just a little, but I'm also sort of intimidated by her. Sure, I have Alex but that might only be because of the star. I'm not sure I'll ever be certain whether either of our feelings are genuine until the star is gone.

I end up staying on the bed until Alex returns. He doesn't look as lost as he did when he walked out. "The sacrifice that I made when we were at the cabin," he sits down on the bed beside me, this time forgetting to leave space between us and our knees touch, "The one with the *memoria extracto*, created a seal in your blood, which prevents Stephan from getting close to you for a certain amount of time, because he was the cause behind the sacrifice."

"Where did you learn that from?"

"Aislin. I guess it's basic magic 101."

"And she never bothered to say anything."

"It's Aislin," he says with a shrug. "She probably didn't even think about it until I brought it up. Although she insists she had an entire conversation with us where she explained it to us."

"That's strange… although, now that you mention it, I can kind of remember it happening." Aislin, Alex, and I in the living room as she's telling us about it; I can picture it pretty clearly, yet it doesn't feel like it really happened. "I think something strange is going on."

"Something strange is always going on." Alex places a hand on my knee, the corners of his lips quirking.

"That's not what I meant." I pause. "It just seems like even though I erased all these events, some of them I can still remember even though technically they never happened."

"I wonder if something happened when you erased time."

"I wouldn't be surprised, since everyone always said simply reading a vision wrong could mess everything up. Plus Nicholas talked about that whole butterfly effect."

He winces at something I said, but quickly composes himself and scoots closer. "How's your stomach feeling?" He reaches for my shirt and without waiting for permission, lifts the hem up to inspect my wound.

"What exactly happened to me?" I ask as he carefully peels back a corner or the bandage.

He releases an unsteady breath. "A piece of glass cut you." He puts the bandage back in place, lowers my shirt, and then brushes his finger across my hairline. "It cut you here, too, but it wasn't too bad. No stitches or anything." There's a trace of a smile and I bet he's thinking about the last time he put stitches on me, which seems like such a long time ago.

"It felt like I was dying." I lightly touch my head.

Fear flashes in his eyes. "You were… did."

"I *died*?"

He nods. "But I brought you back."

"H-how?" I'm so shocked I can hardly speak. Dead. I was dead and now I'm not.

"I have no idea, but we need to be more careful." He reaches out to touch me again, but then pulls back. "We can't let anything happen to you."

I want to ask him why, because of the star or because of me, but either answer would be painful. "Is everyone else okay?" I ask. He doesn't answer, gazing off over my shoulder. "Alex, what happened? Just tell me. Whatever it is I can handle it."

"No, I'm not sure you can," he says. "It's bad."

"It can't be worse than when you died," I tell him. "So yes, I can handle it."

Emotions flicker in his eyes, one's I don't understand. "It's Nicholas...he's dead."

Chapter 9

Dead? Nicholas is dead. The faerie/Foreseer who only hours ago was annoying the shit out of me is gone forever, taking his irritating habits and knowledge of how to fix the world right along with him.

"I'm not sure how to react." I admit, gripping the blanket. "I'm so confused."

"That's understandable," he says concernedly. "Death is confusing."

"Yeah, but I didn't really even like him," I say guiltily.

"Neither did I," he tells me with a sad smile. "But it's still hard to hear of someone dying, maybe even a little frightening."

I let the blanket go from my death grip. "You sound so wise right now."

"I'm always wise." He winks at me, but there's sadness flowing from him. "But I've also lost people to death before. And whether it was my grandmother or the eighty year old lady who lived next door, it was all confusing and painful."

"I'm sorry. I don't know what to say... I've never lost someone. Only thought I did."

His fingers find my cheekbone. Forbidden territory again, but I don't stop him. "And I'm sure thinking it still hurt as much as if it'd happened."

"That's not true," I say, shaking my head. "I couldn't feel when I truly began to understand that my parents were dead, at least according to Marco and Sophia. It didn't hurt, not like when I thought I'd lost you." The last part sort of slips out, falls off my tongue, hangs between us, waiting for someone to pick it up."

"I want to kiss you better," he says in a hoarse voice, eyes fervent with the desire he was talking about in the car. "I do, but..."

"But you can't," I finish for him, our lips inching nearer. I feel the heat of his breath caressing my skin, the warmth of his hand on my thigh practically scalds my skin, and the heat in his eyes, the emotions; it almost makes me okay with dying. Maybe I could, give that up, my life for love and for the world.

I'm about to say that to him, ask him if maybe we should allow ourselves to go to that place if we can, let our hearts beat until they connect, then the star will fade and will go with it too. Sacrifice. It might be the only way.

But I can't seem to get the words to leave my mouth, so I selfishly say something else. "How did he die?"

Alex draws a path up to my eye, then delicately traces a line below it, back and forth... it feels mind-numbingly good. "He was on the side of the impact. I think it killed him instantly."

Reality rushes over me like a bone-crushing wave. Nicholas is gone and I can't save the world, unless I want to die and let Alex die too.

"It's all over." My stomach churns again and I throw my hand over my mouth as I my stomach threatens to dry heave. "Where's the bathroom?"

Alex points over his shoulder at a door on the opposing wall as the one he walked out earlier. "There's one right there."

I jump off the bed and run over to it as Alex gets to his feet, calling out after me. I slam the door, rush over to the toilet, and puke until my stomach is empty. Until everything is empty.

After I rinse my mouth and splash my face with cold water, I take in my reflection in the mirror. I look like death, my violet eyes red and puffy, my skin pallid, and there's a thin cut on my forehead.

"What am I going to do?" The choices I'm facing are tearing me apart. "How am I supposed to decide?"

A knock on the door. "Are you okay in there?" Alex asks.

"Yeah," I say, pulling myself together before I open the door. "I'm just not feeling very well... it must be the accident or something."

He gives sympathetic look. "Do you want to lie down? You've been through a lot of the last few days."

I shake my head and step past him and out of the bathroom. "I want to see Laylen and make sure he's doing okay."

Alex frowns. "He's fine." He leans against the doorframe of the bathroom and points at the door across the room, the one he walked out of earlier. "He's out there with Stasha and Aislin."

I feel a little weird about how much I want to see Laylen and with how uneasy it's making Alex, but I still head out and he trails behind me, keeping his distance. The air smells leafy and reminds me of Nicholas, but it's coming from the plants flourishing from the walls and ceiling. At the end of the hallway is a living room with walls covered in rose wallpaper that match the sofas. Like the bedroom, there are plants all over the shelves, vines decorating the ceiling, and plants in the windowsill. The curtain is open and I can see that it's still dusk.

I glance over my shoulder at Alex and raise my eyebrows. "Okay, the plants are kind of creeping me out."

He shrugs, not agreeing or disagreeing. "The oxygen's good for her or something… but yeah, still kind of creepy." He nods his head to my right. "Everyone's in the kitchen."

I turn and spot Laylen sitting at the kitchen table. Strands of his blond, blue-tipped hair hang in his bright blue eyes, tattoos curve across his arms, including the markings for the Mark of Immortality, and his long legs are stretched out to the side of him as he sits sideways in the chair. Aislin is next to him, her hair damp and she's wearing a white floral dress, opening and closing her hand causing her skin to smoke as if she's practicing a spell. The other person at the table is also in a floral dress; a green one. Her blond hair reminds me of sunshine and sunflowers and her eyes are sky blue. Tan gloves cover her hands and her lips are glossy. I've seen this girl before, not just in a photo back at Laylen's house, but in a vision… or memory... She was holding Aislin's spell book.

"Shit."

"What's wrong?" Alex asks, his breath tickling the back of my neck—I hadn't realized he was so close.

I turn and our lips are only a sliver of space away. "I've seen that girl before," I whisper.

His brow curves upward. "Stasha?"

I nod. "In a vision... or memory... I'm not really sure, but she was holding Aislin's spell book."

Alex doesn't seem as surprised as I am. He simply says, "I'll take care of it." Then he winds around me and heads for the kitchen table.

I turn around and discover Stasha has focused her attention on me, her gaze shooting daggers. "Everything okay?" she asks Alex as he strolls up to her.

"We need to talk," he says, then gestures for her to follow him as he walks toward a door on the far back wall. I don't know where the door leads to, but what I do know is I feel so jealous when the two of them go into the room behind it that I feel like I'm about to ignite into flames.

I need to concentrate on something else besides this jealous feeling festering inside me so I look at Laylen. He's fiddling with his lip ring, sucking on it sexily as he draws it between his teeth and watching him do it turns out to be a great distraction.

He catches my eye and a look of relief washes over him. Without saying a word, he rises from the chair and crosses the room in three long strides, catching me by the elbow and guiding me into the living room with him, leaving Aislin alone in the kitchen to practice her magic.

We stand face to face between the sofas and I'm so relieved to see him, it takes me a moment to find my voice.

"How are you doing?" I finally ask.

"I don't know... Okay, I guess."

"You had me worried... I still am."

"I know you are," he says, meeting my gaze, almost looking glad that I'm worried about him, but maybe it's because he hardly has anyone in his life. "I'm sorry. I just freaked out when your mom told me this was done on purpose to me." He gestures at himself and then the mark on his arm, indicating he's referring to being a vampire. "I didn't do anything, though... I didn't bite anyone... I wanted to... so fucking badly." He chews on his bottom lip, staring at the spot on my neck where he bit me once. "I kept having dreams of drinking your blood and I swear I could taste it... it was maddening."

"I thought it was getting easier to control?"

"It was... but then something changed inside me... and it felt like I went back to the place that I started if that makes any sense."

I have to wonder if maybe this has something to do with me resetting time. "It's going to be okay," I say, repeating my father's words, even though I'm not positive I believe them. "And if this ever gets to be too much, you can talk to me. You and I are in this together." I look directly him in the eye. "Promise me you won't run away again. That no matter what happens or what you're feeling, you'll come to me first."

He nods and then pulls me in for a hug, breathing in my sent as he puts his lips up to my neck and presses a kiss there. "I'm so sorry... For thinking about you the way that I do."

My veins are filled with liquid fire beneath my skin. It's so wrong, but every time I think about his fangs sinking into me, I feel like moaning. "It's okay," I say. "Everything's going to be okay."

But I'm not sure if it is.

About ten minutes later, Alex and Stasha emerge from the back room, Alex looking annoyed and Stasha looking pissed. Alex strides over to the kitchen table and drops a thick, leather book right in front of Aislin.

"Found your spell book," Alex says, shaking his head in annoyance as he narrows his eyes at Stasha. "Apparently someone's been sneaking around."

"I wasn't sneaking around," Stasha retorts, crossing her arms. "You were right there when you saw me take it."

"No I wasn't," he argues as Aislin hugs the book to her chest.

"Yes, you were," Stasha insists, stepping toward him. "You were in the beach house and she," she aims a finger at me, "Was possessed by the devil himself."

"You mean Stephan?" I ask. "But I thought—"

"It's time to go," Alex interrupts in a clipped tone. "We've got a lot of shit to take care of."

I want to ask him questions, starting with the fact that Stasha can remember a point in time that technically never occurred. And also why she stole the spell book for Stephan, which would mean she is… was helping him. But he looks so angry that I decide just to go with the flow until we get out of Stasha's house.

When Aislin and Alex join us in the living room, we get ready to leave via transportation even though Aislin is worried about taking four people. But she said she'd try, I think just to get us the hell out of there.

She has a black candle lit as she sits on the floor with a crystal in her hand. I go to take my necklace off, to avoid repelling Aislin's magic back on her, when I realize it is missing.

"Wait, where's my necklace?" I touch the base of my neck, panicking.

"I took it off when Aislin transported us here," Alex tells me, still aggravated. "I left it on the nightstand in the room you were in when you woke up."

I hurry to the bedroom to get it, but the necklace isn't on the nightstand like Alex said. I search the bedroom floor, in the bed, under the bed, inside the closet. I even check the bathroom, but no luck.

I really don't want to be the girl who cries over a lost piece of jewelry, but I might be if I don't find it—it has sentimental value.

"Looking for this?"

The sound of her catlike voice sends the hairs on the back of my neck on end. I slowly turn toward the doorway where Stasha is standing, her glove-covered hand up in front of her, a shiny, silver object dangling from her finger.

My locket.

"Why do you have that?" I put up my guard, knowing that something isn't right.

With a sardonic grin, she shakes her head as she lowers her hand. "I know girls like you." She struts into the room, swinging the necklace around her finger. "Sad. Lonely. *Pathetic*. God, I can't believe Alex would even have the slightest bit of interest in you."

I let girls like Stasha walk all over me back in high school. Of course I couldn't feel anything at the time so it didn't matter then, but now it's pissing me off. I shove Stasha back with more force than I mean to and she trips back and lands on her ass. As she sits there in shock, I snatch the necklace away from her and then run out of the room before she can take one of those gloves off her hand and kill me. I don't make it very far down the hall, though, before her fingers wraps around my ankle. She yanks on my leg, sending me flat on my face. I kick my foot at her, but miss repeatedly, so instead start dragging myself across the floor in this weird arm crawl way.

I glance over my shoulder and realize it's not Stasha that has a hold of me but her plants. The vines that cover everything have taken on their own life and are snaking around trying to get a hold of me. They are alive and writhing all over the place like snakes.

119

Stasha walks through them toward me and I open my mouth to yell for help, but another vine clamps down on my mouth, silencing me and then others ravel around my body, making it impossible to move.

She kneels down in front of me as I struggle to get free. "You should know better than to mess with someone like me," she says, tugging off one of her gloves. Then she reaches for me, ready to touch me, ready to kill.

I fight with all my strength, but it's useless so I decide to go another route. I shut my eyes and picture the sandy shore outside the beach house, just enough of a distance away that the *Praesidium* won't interfere with my power. I can hear the ocean waves colliding with the shore, see the moon shining in the starry sky, feel the salty breeze kissing my cheeks.

"What are you doing?" Stasha asks, but her voice is muffled, fading.

Take me there, I think, feeling the sand touch my toes.

But then a hand grabs my arm and I feel nothing but fire.

Chapter 10

My face slams into the sand. I quickly scramble to my feet and sprint into the ocean to dunk my arm into the water, expecting relief from the fiery pain, but only receiving more pain. I let out a jaw-clenched scream as I run for the beach house just up the shore. The pain is unbearable, but what hurts even worse is what it represents. Stasha touched me with her bare hands. Am I going to drop dead at any moment?

By the time I reach the back door of the house, I'm about to vomit from the sensation of death in my arm. I fling open the back door and fumble around in the dark until I find the light switch. The lights flip on and I stumble over to the sink, turn on the faucet, and submerge my arm underneath the cold, salt-free water.

It feels a little bit better and I stand let the water flow over it, catching my breath as I wait for the pain to subside. It begins to dwindle, but olive-green marks start to appear on my veins, forming vinery.

I touch the lines with my fingertip and cringe. "Is this permanent?"

I wait a little longer with my arm in the water, hoping they'll fade, but they don't. Finally I give up and put my locket on right as I hear a soft *poof* from inside the living room. Not sure what it's from, I tiptoe to the doorway and peer around the corner. A purple haze fills the room and Alex, Laylen, and Aislin are in the center it. As soon as they all see me, they're worried expressions relax.

Aislin drops the crystal and candle on the table, but keeps hold of her spell book. "Thank God," she says as she flops tiredly. "I thought she killed you."

"What happened?" Alex crosses the room with his arms open, as if he's going to hug me, but by the time he reaches me, he's changed his mind and lowered them to his side.

I extend my arm out to him, showing him the lines mapping my veins. "Her plants attacked me and then she touched me....you know, you could have warned me about the plants."

He curses under his breath then examines my arm, running his thumb up and down the lines. "Dammit, she's fucking crazy."

"Yes, she is," I agree. "It's not permanent, is it? Please, please, tell me it's going to go away."

Alex looks up at me, remorseful. "I'm sorry, Gemma. I never should have taken you there."

I sigh, removing my arm from his grasp. "Great. Now I'm always going to have a reminder of when your ex-girlfriend tried to kill me."

I don't know who laughs first, but suddenly we are all laughing as if I've just said the best joke in the world. Sleep deprivation is a funny thing, I guess, and makes everyone kind of loopy.

After the laughter settles down, we gather around the coffee table, putting the mapping ball on it, the light in the center illuminating a ghostly glow. I start to get up to look for my mother but Aislin tells me that right before they transported here she got a call from my mom, saying that she ran to the gas station to pick up some food, because no one had really been stocking the cupboards. So I sit back down and we quickly explain to Laylen what's been going on and then we start discussing how Stasha got the book.

"So Stasha took the book, but it took place in a time that was erased, yet it still happened," Alex states as he kicks his foot up on his knee and rests his arm on the back of the sofa, just behind me.

"It sounds so confusing when you put it like that," I say. "But yeah, I think that's what happened."

"But how?" Aislin wonders as she flips through her spell book. She's been doing it since we sat down, I think looking for some sort of signs Stasha did something to it.

"I have no idea." I pause. "Nicholas would have, but unfortunately he's... gone."

We all grow quiet for a moment, thinking about what happened. I wonder if he'll get a funeral, if the fey mourn like humans, or if they do something else.

"We need to make a plan." Aislin changes the subject as she closes her spell book.

"Thanks for clarifying the obvious, Aislin," Alex says sarcastically.

Aislin rolls her eyes. "Don't be an ass."

"What we need to do is go to the City of Crystal." I pick up the mapping ball and rotate it in my hands. "So I can get inside this thing and fix the vision and hopefully all this other stuff that's gotten out of place will be fixed too."

"Why do you think your father would reset time, if it was going to mess it up?" Laylen asks with a pucker at his brow. "It doesn't make any sense."

It gets quiet again, but a different kind of quiet, one where I know they're all thinking the same thing, but too afraid to say it.

Finally, Alex gets the balls to put it out there. "Gemma, you don't think he's setting you up, do you?

To maybe finish whatever it is he started with my father."

"Who said he was doing something with your father," I say coldly. "He never said anything about that."

"He never said much about anything," Alex points out, his knuckles grazing the back of my neck, as if he's attempting to keep me calm with his touch. "But I'm guessing that he probably erased the vision and recreated things so the world would end for my father."

"Stop saying that," I snap defensively.

He gives me a look of empathy. "Gemma, I get defending your father, trust me, I really do. But sometimes what we want them to be isn't what they are."

"Shut up," I snap, surprising everyone in the room. "You don't know anything about him, and you're making judgments based on one thing."

"No one knows anything about him." Alex's hand drifts to my shoulder.

But I shrug it off and get to my feet. "I need some air." I hurry for the door and burst outside. I hear Aislin say something about let her go as I shut the door behind me. Then I sink down on the front steps, bring my knees to my chest, rest my chin on them and stare at the stars.

"Are you evil?" I wonder aloud, wishing to hear his voice again, but the only answer I get is silence and that leaves me wondering if maybe Alex is right. Perhaps my dad is working with Stephan to end the world and using me to help him.

Chapter 11

After staring at the stars for an eternity, I come to the conclusion that what I need to do is see the vision my father changed and make the decision for myself whether he's working for the evil side or the good one. If what he's told me is true, it should be clear in the vision. If not, then I won't change it. However, that still leaves the problems of getting into the mapping ball.

I march into the house and pick it up from the coffee table, all three of them staring at me as if they think I'm having a meltdown. "I'm going to do this—I have to. If anything looks suspicious then I won't change the vision, but I need to see it for myself."

Alex is already shaking his head before I even finish. He stands up, reaching to take the crystal ball from my hand, but I put it behind my back. "You don't even know how to use it," he says. "Nicholas never explained anything to you other than how to get enough power to use it."

"Well, I can start by getting the power from the City of Crystal," I tell him. "And then go from there."

"It's too risky," Alex says. "Hell, sneaking into the City of Crystal is risky enough not to mention stealing some of the power, bringing it back—which I might add we don't know how to do—and then you've got to figure out how to use the power to get inside that thing."

"Maybe there's another Foreseer we can ask," Aislin suggests, glancing at her phone as it vibrates. "There has to be one that might help us, right? Nicholas couldn't be the only one."

"Involving another Foreseer would mean involving another person, which is risky," Alex says. "Besides, we don't even know what side the Foreseers are on."

"Maybe you could ask your father," Laylen says to me. "I mean, you've been there once, so why can't you go there again? You could also maybe get more of a feel if he's..." He stops talking, offering me an apologetic look.

"I don't know if I can... when I went there the first time it was entirely by accident and he wouldn't tell me anything no matter how much I asked him," I say, sitting down on the coffee table and studying the crystal ball, still illuminating from the center star. "I think I need to talk to my mom. She might know something that could help." I check the clock on the wall, realizing it's nearing morning. "I'm starting to get worried about her... Shouldn't she be back by now?" I look at Aislin for an explanation.

"I don't know...maybe she had to go somewhere else besides the store." She shrugs, but it's a blasé shrug, like she doesn't care, or knows something else she's not telling me.

"What's going on?" I ask. "You've been acting weird every time I bring up my mother."

Aislin presses her lips together, looking everywhere but at me. "She's fine."

"I didn't ask if she was fine," I tell her sternly. "I asked what's going on."

Again she refuses to speak, so Alex intervenes, "What exactly did she say on the phone?" he asks his sister.

Aislin shakes her head, her lips starting to quiver. "I don't know. I don't remember."

"Aislin," Alex warns, stepping toward her. "What did she say?"

"I don't want to tell you!" Aislin cries, dropping her head into her hands to hide her tears. "If I do then you'll just go and try to save her, and I can't take any more of it!"

"Any more of what?" Alex's voice softens a smidgeon.

"You risking your life all the time." She lifts her head back up and her eyes are red from the tears. "Dad's crazy, mom left, and you're all I have left. I mean, I get that it's our job and everything to protect the world but seriously I need a god damn break... You've already died once."

"You can remember that?" Alex and I say simultaneously.

She nods, her face contorted with confusion as she dabs tears from her cheeks and eyes with her fingertips. "Yeah... I actually can as of now."

Alex and I trade a look. "Something strange is going on," he says.

"It has to be from me altering the vision," I utter quietly, knowing it makes my father look even guiltier.

"Then we need to either fix it," he says firmly. "Or find out what's going on."

I hold the crystal ball up. "That's what I'm trying to do, but Aislin needs to tell me where my mom is. She might be the only one who can help us at the moment."

Alex gives me a tolerant look, like he doesn't want to do what he does next. Still he sits down beside Aislin and puts his arm around her shoulder. "Look, I get where you're coming from, but this is what I—we do. You've known that since we were three years old and father explained to us that we were Keepers. We risk our lives and that's how things are. So please, just tell Gemma where her mother is."

She shakes her head again. "I'm not going to, so you can stop pretending to be nice."

"You can tell me," I offer to Aislin. "I'll go get her by myself."

"He won't let you." She scowls in her brother's direction. "He's too stubborn and cares for you too much."

"I won't tell him," I say and in return get the nastiest look from Alex. "I'll keep it a secret and use my Foreseer power to go there by myself."

Rage flares in Alex's eyes as he rises to his feet, tall and sturdy, intimidating, but I refuse to back down. "Like hell I'm going to—"

I stand up and put my hand over his mouth, ignoring the warmth of his lips against my flesh. "If I foresee there, he doesn't have a choice. You can have a tantrum but in the end, you can't make me take you." I lower my hand and wait for him to argue, because by the expression on his face, I can tell that he's going to.

His eyes darken and his voice drops to a firm, husky tone. "I can always tie you to the bed and make it so you can't go anywhere."

He's right. There's *Praesidium* all over this place, making it impossible for me to use my Foreseer power inside it. And he's strong enough that all he'd have to do is pick me up and carry be to the bed—he could tie me down with one hand. And by the amount of intensity in his eyes, I can tell that he wants to do it and by the way my blood is heating beneath my skin, I think part of me wants him to do it too.

Laylen finally clears his throat, alleviating the tension. "I can go with her."

"That doesn't make me feel any better," Alex says, displeased. "I need to be the one to go with her."

"Laylen can protect me just as much as you can," I tell him, which is clearly the wrong thing to say.

"Like fucking hell he can." He leans in and puts his lips beside my ear. "Would he die for you?"

I squeeze my eyes shut as my heart starts to pound. This is not good. Emotions. They're surfacing, so many of them, and he can feel it too because his lips graze my neck. "Alex, I think it might be good if Laylen goes with me," I say, breathless. "Not just for Aislin's sake, but for you and me as well."

132

"Gemma... I—"

"It's for the best," I cut him off.

He stiffens. When he pulls back, he gives me a look of indifference. "Fine, if that's what you want."

"It's what I want." But it isn't really. I want him, but I can't have him. Not anymore.

As he steps away from me, I breathe freely again and then turn to Aislin. "Okay, tell me where she is."

She sniffs back more tears. "She went to the Keepers' castle to try and kill my father."

Chapter 12

At first I think I didn't hear her right because why would my mom do such a crazy, erratic, impulsive, dangerous thing? It's crazy—she would have to be crazy.

"Oh my God. She's fucking crazy," I whisper in shock. "She's completely lost her mind... It has to be because she spent all those years in The Underworld, right?"

"She's not crazy," Alex reassures me, putting a hand on my arm as I slowly lower myself onto the sofa. "She just wants to protect you and she probably thought this was the best way not to get you involved, which I completely understand."

"She's going to get herself killed," I state in disbelief. After all these years without a mother, I finally get her back only for her to run straight into danger two days later.

Alex massages my shoulder. "We'll go get her."

"No *we* won't," I say to him, leaning out of his touch. "I will. Stephan doesn't need both of us showing up there so we end up right in his hands where he can lock us up and let the events of the world play out just like he wants them to. It would be like handing him the end of the world on a golden platter. And besides, I made a promise to Aislin that you wouldn't go."

He shakes his head, dumbfounded. "You actually think I'm going to let you go to the Keepers' castle by yourself? Have you seriously learned nothing about me?"

"I've learned you're a stubborn asshole who gets his way all the time," I dare say.

He gives me that dark, lustful look again. "Should we go back to the plan where I tie you up to the bed."

As his gaze sweeps across my body, my skin tingles. "I'll never forgive you if you don't let me go. Like we planned, Laylen will go with me and protect me." I look at Laylen, feeling Alex's demanding gaze burning a hole in the back of my head. "Are you ready to go?" I ask Laylen. "Or, if you don't want to anymore, I understand. I know you offered before you knew where we were going."

Laylen looks at me like I'm acting ridiculous. The he gets to his feet, coming over to me. "Of course, I'm going to go with you."

"Thank you." I almost give him a hug, but decide against it, considering how Alex is acting right now.

"But you should change into some pants first."
Laylen points at the shorts I have on. "It's freezing up
there at night."

I glance at the window where sunlight sparkles
across the land. "But it's morning."

"It's night at the castle," he says. "Trust me."

"Okay, give me a second." I start for the hallway
and go into the bedroom. I put on a pair of jeans,
change my shirt, and rinse my face off, trying to fight
my nerves. I'm going to the castle, where Stephan
could potentially be and I'm not a Keeper or a ninja
warrior. I'm kind of klutzy and uncoordinated. I wonder
what the odds of me walking away unscratched from
this are.

As I'm telling myself to suck it up and think of my
mom, someone knocks on the door.

"Come in," I call out as I pull my long, brown hair
up in a ponytail.

Alex walks in and stuffs his hands into his pockets, glancing around at the room and then the bed
where we've had hot, steamy. "You about ready to
go?"

"Yeah, I think so," I say, reaching for my jacket on
the bedpost, my hand noticeably shaking from my
nerves.

"Hey." He catches my trembling fingers in his hand. "Come here." He guides me with him as he sits down on the bed.

I notice that he's carrying the Sword of Immortality, the jagged blade glinting in the light. I'm about to ask him why he has it when he starts talking.

"My mom left when I was about five," he says, stroking the back of my hand. "At least, I think she left... I have to wonder now, after everything my father has done, if maybe he had something to do with it and if maybe she's dead."

There was so much suffering in his voice and I want to tell him that that probably isn't the case, that I'm sure his mother is okay and that his father had nothing to do with it. But we'd both know I was lying because there's a good chance that might be the case, considering all the horrible things Stephan has done.

"There's this rock at the back of the castle that hides a secret entryway to the basement," he tells me in a state of self-torture. "Laylen should be able to lift the rock up so you guys can get in... no one knows it's there but me." He hands me the Sword of Immortality. "And this will hopefully protect you if you run into my father."

I take the sword from him, feeling the heavy weight of it. "You're giving me something that might kill your father?"

He shrugs, his eyes swimming in a sea of pain. "I want you to be able to protect yourself—you're what's most important." He pauses. "But can you promise me something? That if anything happens at all, if anything even remotely bad looks like it will happen, you'll come right back."

I place the sword on the floor beside my feet. "Alex, I can't—"

He places a hand over my mouth like I did to him earlier. "I know you feel like you need to save her. And I completely understand that. But you also need to understand that you might be the one person who can save the world. So if it all comes down to it, you're going to have to save yourself." I know there is more to it than that, but he isn't going to say it.

So I nod, giving him what he wants, even though it's not the truth. "Okay, I promise."

He lowers his hand from my lips and starts tapping his foot against the floor. "I should be the one going with you."

"No, you shouldn't. Aislin needs you. I—I didn't know that about your mother. No one should be alone in the world."

It gets quiet and my thoughts drift back to my old life filled with loneliness and desolation. All those years with no one. All those years feeling empty. All those years where I didn't know there was so much more to life. Heartache. Longing. Happiness. Sadness. God, there's so much more. And as dangerous as my new life is, I would never trade it back. I never want to go back to that ever. I just hope I get the chance to live life without the star.

"Gemma," Alex says almost as if he's in pain as he slants toward me. "I can't help myself... when it comes to you and putting you in harm's way it's like I have to fight this desperate compulsion to save you. It's why I gave you the locket, why I tried to run from my father, why I intercepted the *memoria extracto*, why I stabbed myself with a needle and killed myself to bring you back. I know you erased the last part, but I'd do it again in a heartbeat."

I want to point out that now he's remembering things that never technically happened again, but he silences me with a brush of his lips. It starts out innocent, but when my hands slide up the front of his lean chest, he grabs onto my hips as his tongue slides deep into my mouth and he lays me back on the bed. He tastes like mint and smells like cologne, his body bringing me warmth as it covers mine. My back arches into him as my insides quiver with need. I feel out of control in a forbidden way.

"Alex," I say breathlessly as his hand travels up my shirt toward my breast. "We have to stop... it's becoming too... too..." I groan as his hand wanders un-under my bra and he pinches my nipple. "Much..."

"I know." He groans against my mouth as he cups my breast. "But it's so fucking hard." His body falls between my legs and I grind up against him.

"But we're going to end up killing each other..." Another grind of my hips and then another. God, I'd almost take being dead just to feel this one more time. "If we don't stop..." I know what I am putting out there, that we were heading toward feelings of love. It is a blunt move on my part, but it gets him to stop.

He pushes back, looking down at me, an arm on each side of my head. "I know." His brow's furrow at his own words. Then he gets up and leaves the room as if nothing happened.

***

Everyone decides it's best to clear out the *Praesidium* for the moment, so that I can foresee in the privacy of the house. Alex takes care of it while I head for the living room. Laylen gives me a wary look when I walk out into the living room, carrying the Sword of

Immortality, as if I might do something stupid like trip over my feet and stab him.

"You sure you should be carrying that?" he questions with amusement and a bit of fear. He's changed his clothes, but is still wearing his typical black jeans and shirt, studded belt and leather wrist band, and boots.

"I promise I'll be super careful," I say with as much humor as I can muster up. "And try not to stab you."

"Gee thanks," he teases, nudging me with his shoulder, seeming more at ease then he did at Stasha's house.

I smile at him and start to shut my eyes, telling my heart to calm down as I get ready to foresee us out of here

"Wait!"

My eyes open as Aislin comes running into the room and stops in front of me. "I have something for you to help you see in the dark."

I think she's going to give me a flashlight or a lantern, but instead she whispers, "*luvo vos animadverto*," under her breath, then she puts her hand in front of her mouth and blows something sparkly in my face.

I drop the sword on the ground in reaction and press my hands against my eyes. "Oh my God! What the hell was that?"

"Oh shit, I'm sorry. I probably should have warned you first," Aislin apologizes. "I was just so excited that I finally figured out how to do the spell correctly."

I rub my eyes and blink against the burning sensation. "Okay, what spell was it though?"

She beams. "Night vision." She dusts her hands off. "So you don't have to stumble around in the dark blindly when you get to the castle."

"What about Laylen?" I ask, picking up the sword from off the floor.

"He doesn't need it," she tells me, giving Laylen a once over, looking at him in a way that I look at Alex sometimes and I remember how she told me they use to date. I wonder if she still has feelings for him? "He already has night vision."

Laylen doesn't reciprocate the look, I think still carrying around too much pain from her abandoning him in his time of need. "We should go," he says and Aislin looks hurt. "Are you sure you're going to be okay with this thing?" he asks, nodding at the sword. "It just about landed on my foot."

I thread my fingers through Laylen's and take a deep breath. "I've got this. Trust me." I actually sound confident, although I don't feel that way.

I don't bother looking at Alex, knowing it'll make it harder to leave. But I can feel him watching me from across the room, arms folded, as he sinks into the shadows. Then I shut my eyes and do what I need to do. I picture the lake, the forest circling it, the grey-stone castle in the background. And then suddenly I'm falling with Laylen by my side.

Chapter 13

I manage to land without falling, but that might be because I use Laylen's arm for support. Once we're both settled on the ground out in the forest just a little ways from the castle, I glance up at the sky. The full moon shines vividly, silver speckles of stars and the darkness surrounds us, but I can see as clearly as if it were day.

"Amazing," I say, touching the corner of my eye.

"Pretty cool, huh?" Laylen states, playfully prodding me in the side.

I nod, lowering my hand. Silence encloses us and for a moment we just stare at each other, feelings connected to the bite attempting to fight to the surface. *We're alone.*

"We should get going," I finally say.

He nods, unable to take his eyes off me. "Yeah, we should."

I nod again and then start hiking through the trees toward the castle and Laylen follows my lead. Twigs and leaves crunch under our shoes, the cool air nips at my skin, and the silence is driving me mad.

"Why did you go to Stasha's?" I ask, attempting to break the silence. "She doesn't seem like a very good person."

"Yeah, but neither am I."

"Don't say that," I tell him. "You're a good person. You're here with me and you don't have to be."

His expression is guarded. "Maybe I have an alternative motive." His gaze flicks to my neck where my pulse is throbbing.

"Don't do that," I say. "Don't pretend you're bad because you think everyone thinks you are."

He gives me a hard look but then sighs. "I was standing outside of the Red Dragon, debating whether I wanted to go in or not, when Stasha showed up out of the blue. I think she hangs out there sometimes, but she didn't want to admit it, so she pretended to be wandering around the area. She asked me if I wanted to go back to her house and I went with her because the only other option I had was going inside the Red Dragon."

I zip up my jacket. "Well, I'm glad you left with her then, even if she is a lunatic."

He chuckles and for a split second, some of his pain alleviates. "That she is."

145

"You know, Aislin was upset the whole time you were gone," I tell him. "She cried a lot."

"Aislin always cries," Laylen says, shoving a branch blocking his path. "She's been that way forever."

"Yeah, I know, but she still cares about you. I can tell."

"I know."

"Have you... Have you ever thought about forgiving her?"

He shakes his head. "I'm not ready to do that yet."

I nod. "Okay, I understand."

"What about you? Did you cry while I was gone?" he asks it casually, but his tone portrays the mere opposite. Tension builds and the vein on my neck throbs. I can't help but think about what it feels like when he sinks his fangs into my skin... drinks my blood... sheer ecstasy.

"Oh, yeah, I cried until my tears ran out," I joke, trying to break the tension. "In fact, I locked myself in my room and refused to leave until someone found you."

He's reluctant at first to go with the joke but gives in and smiles. "I knew you secretly had feelings for me. I'm glad you finally admitted it."

I laugh and he swings his arm around me, pulling me close to him. "Honestly, I could be okay with this." He brushes his lips across the top of my forehead, spreading heat to my toes, but a different kind of heat than Alex's touch brings. What that means, though, I have no idea. "Just you and me."

Part of me agrees with him that I could stay like this forever. Just Laylen and me. No electricity reminding me of what I was and what I could never be. No worry about falling in love with someone that could lead to my death and his. Life would be simpler if I just fell in love with Laylen and he loved me back. The problem is, though, I know from the silence on the back of my neck that it isn't happening, at least not at this moment.

As we reach the edge of the forest, Laylen steers us behind a large oak tree as the lights glowing from the castle windows light up the dark. "Okay, we're probably just going to have to make a run for the back." He peeks around the corner of the tree trunk and out into the area in front of the castle, which is a long, wide, stretch of grass, where anyone can see us if they're looking out. "I don't see anyone outside… And I think I see the rock Alex was talking about." He looks over his shoulder at me. "Are you sure you're ready for this? Because I can just do it. It might be better for you to stay here."

I shake my head. "No way. She's my mom and this is my thing. I need to do this. Everyone's always taking care of me and protecting me all the time and I'm getting tired of it. Besides," I raise the sword, "I have this."

He inches back from the sharp tip of the blade. "Alright, then let's go."

We charge out from the trees and race across the dewy grass toward the castle. I trip over a rock, and catch myself, but Laylen takes that as a cue that I need help. He grabs me by the arm and effortlessly lifts me up and throws me onto his back.

"I should have done this in the first place," he says, then speeds up so fast that everything becomes blurry and incoherent. I try to keep the sword away from him for the rest of the journey, holding my breath for most of the way and only breathe freely again when he stops and sets me back down on the ground in front of a gigantic rock.

"I'm guessing this is it," Laylen says, then presses his hands to the rock and easily shoves it aside. Beneath it is a hole burrowing deep into the ground. Even with my night vision, I can't see the bottom.

"How far of a drop is it?" I wonder, leaning over cautiously and peering down into it.

He shrugs. "There's only one way to find out." Then without warning, he jumps down into it.

"Laylen," I hiss, kneeling down by the edge. "Are you okay?"

"Go ahead and jump," he calls out. "It's not too far and I'll catch you."

I glance back at the castle and the trees, then slide my legs into the hole. Without any hesitation, I jump in, knowing if I dither, I'll psych myself out. Gripping onto the sword handle, I fall into the darkness, but not for too long and then I'm safe in Laylen's arms.

"Holy shit," I breathe against his chest as I clasp my arms tightly around his neck and squeeze my legs against his hips. "That was nerve racking."

His hands are tense on my waist. "Yeah... I guess so..." His fingers shift downward and dig into my hips. As his head leans in, his lips brush the crook of my neck. Before I can stop him, he's kissing my flesh, his tongue sliding out and his teeth grazing but not entering. For a moment I let him, because it feels so good and I feel like a complete asshole when he's the one that pulls away.

"Sorry," he says, setting me down quickly. "It's just that you smelled so good and I... maybe we should just go back and I'll come here by myself."

"Laylen, it's fine." I find his arm in the dark. Either my night vision stopped working or there's nothing around us but dark. "I know you won't hurt me." Which is true. His bite doesn't hurt at all.

"Alright." He pulls his hand out from my touch and looks left then right.

"Can you see?" I ask. "Because I can't."

"Barely." With reluctance, he takes my hand and leads me with him as he descends into a dark tunnel that seems to go on forever. Just when I start to think that there's no end to it, it opens up to a room. But I instantly want to shrink back into the dark tunnel again at the sight in front of me. A torture chamber with chains and whips and bars. And in the center of it all, fastened to a rack, is a girl.

Chapter 14

"What is this place?" I whisper, staring at the girl who appears to either be asleep or unconscious. She has to be only about eighteen or nineteen, younger than me.

Laylen shakes his head, his eyes skimming the chains hanging from the ceiling. "I have no idea... I've never been down here before."

"Should we..." I motion at the girl bound by ropes to the rack. "Should we free her?"

Laylen looks skeptical but slowly makes his way over to her. I follow closely at his heels. The girl looks dead, eyes sealed, her body still.

"Is she... is she alive?" I ask Laylen as he examines her.

He assesses the ropes around her wrists and ankles. "Yeah, I can hear her heart beating."

"Should we..." I move my hand for one of the ropes that's around her wrist. "Should I untie her?"

Laylen hesitates then nods, extending his hand for the rope around her other wrist. The rack isn't stretching her limbs to their full capacity, but her skin is pulled tight and shows each one of her bones. Her curly black hair is matted and looks like it hasn't been washed in ages. Her blue dress is faded and frayed and she isn't wearing any shoes.

She remains still as Laylen and I untie her wrists and ankles and she doesn't budge even when she's free, her eyes staying shut as she breathes in and out softly.

"Maybe she's—" I start to say, but then the girl's eyes open.

She looks at us then pulls her arms in and bends her knees as she leaps from the rack and backs herself up into the corner where an array of whips hang from the wall.

"It's okay," Laylen says with his hands up in front of him. "We're not going to—" She lets out a blood curdling scream and Laylen rushes for her. "Son of a..." Laylen grabs her as gently as possible and covers her mouth with his hand. "We're not going to hurt you, but you have got to stop screaming."

The girl's bright yellow, cat-like eyes scan the room, the rack, the stairway that goes to a door, panting profusely, then land on me. She grabs onto Laylen's arms and draws them down so his hand uncovers her mouth.

"It's you," she says in amazement. "I can't believe it."

"Yeah, it's me." I give Laylen an is-she-crazy look and he shrugs, unsure.

"You think you know her?" he asks her.

She nods, slipping from his arms and taking a step toward me, but Laylen gets nervous and places himself in between us. "She's the one he talks about all the time. The girl with the violet eyes—the star."

"Stephan told you about me?" I ask, peering over Laylen's shoulder at the girl.

She glances apprehensively at the top of the spiral stairs and then nods. "Yes, the man with the scar."

"Why are you here?" Laylen wonders. "Does he have you trapped?"

She cocks her head to the side, examining me over with her unnatural yellow eyes. "I'm the half faerie, half Keeper he needs for his plan, so he told me I had to live here." She motions at the torture chamber we're in. "This is my home—where I was raised." She turns around in a circle, looking at everything. "But it's okay..." she says it as if she's trying to convince herself. "Because I'm his daughter."

Chapter 15

Time freezes. No one moves, talks, breathes. At first I think I've heard her wrong, but then I see the shock on Laylen's face and realize I must be correct, which leaves me wondering if Aislin and Alex know about her.

"No, there's no way." Laylen shakes his head in denial. "Aislin and Alex don't have a sister."

"I'm only their half-sister." She talks strangely, as if conversing is foreign to her. "And they don't know about me. My father keeps me hidden all the time. Down here." She gestures at the rack. "This is kind of like my bed." She says it as if she's oblivious to the fact that it's so warped and wrong.

"Of course he does," Laylen mutters, disgusted.

"Why would he keep you hidden?" I ask, moving around to Laylen's side.

"Keepers aren't supposed to mix like that with fey," Laylen explains to me, his attention focused on the girl untrustingly. "There's something about the blood… too much mythical creature on one side and not enough on the other that creates an imbalance."

He discretely nods his head at the girl and lowers his voice. "It makes things a little off."

"Yeah, I can see that," I say, then turn to the girl. "What's your name?"

She sticks out her hand awkwardly to shake Laylen's hand. "I'm Aleesa."

Laylen shakes her hand politely. "Nice to meet you Aleesa."

I eye over Aleesa's yellow eyes, dark hair, sharp features and something doesn't add up. "You don't look like them. Alex and Aislin, I mean."

"Oh, I get my looks from my mother. She was fey," she says, like it explains everything.

"Many of the fey have bright yellow eyes and dark hair like hers," Laylen adds. "Nicholas was an exception."

"So Stephan's your father," I state still in a state of disbelief.

She nods, tucking one of her tangled curls behind her ear. "I am the half-faerie, half-Keeper sacrifice he needs. I am what will bind the fey to him."

My eyes widen. "The sacrifice."

"Yep," she says simply with her hands behind her back as she rocks forward on her heels.

"How long have you been down here?" I ask.

Her face twists with complexity. "I'm not sure. Forever, I think."

I shudder, feeling sorry for her. "What about your mom? Where's she?"

"Oh, she's gone," she says with a shrug. "She left me because I'm an abomination."

I thought my life had been bad, but I think hers tops mine. At least I wasn't locked up and tortured for god sakes and it proves just how morbid Stephan is; to do this to his own daughter.

"Laylen can I talk to you for just a second?" I back toward the tunnel, motioning him to follow me.

He does, looking confused. "What's wrong?"

"What are we going to do with her?" I whisper, glancing at Aleesa. "We can't just leave here."

He looks back at Aleesa, who's fiddling with a hole in the hem of her worn-out dress. "I guess take her with us." He shrugs.

"But is she...I don't know... She seems a little off. What if she flips out on us or something?" I feel bad for saying it, but it needs to be discussed, if nothing else to prepare ourselves.

"I could flip out on you and yet you're still with me."

"Yeah, but you're you. I trust you more than I trust anyone."

"Maybe you shouldn't."

I sigh and press a kiss to his scruffy cheek. "We'll take her with us. But just keep an eye on her, okay?" I start to head back for Aleesa, but pause, an emotion arising inside me, one that I think means Laylen and I are becoming good friends and that I truly care about him. "And I'll always trust you, Laylen. I'll trust you forever."

***

Getting Aleesa to leave with us is a difficult task. She keeps saying over and over again that she isn't allowed to go anywhere outside of the torture chamber. But after some persuading, she finally agrees.

We go up the staircase to the door that Aleesa tells us leads to the inside of the castle. When we approach the top, I realize just how bad my palms are sweating.

"Okay," Laylen says as he grabs the doorknob. "Everyone be on guard."

I nod, clutching onto the sword handle, my legs shaking like a fawn learning how to walk. Laylen cracks the door open and withdraws a small knife out of the back pocket of his jeans as he looks out.

Then he lowers the knife and turns to us. "It seems the secret entrance has led us to yet another secret entrance."

"Really?" I ask as we cautiously step out into a slender hallway. "Are we inside the walls?"

Laylen traces his fingers along the wood paneling. "I think so."

Aleesa hums quietly behind me as we continue down the hallway. The ceiling is low and the walls are decorated with childish art. I sketch my fingers along the drawings of stick people, houses, flowers. Why do I remember this? Each one gives me a sense of familiarity.

Then suddenly it comes violently rushing back to me, a memory once forgotten, or erased from my mind. *Alex and I as children, running up and down the hall, drawing on the walls, laughing, playing.* I can almost hear the giggles haunting the hallway now.

"You okay?" Laylen asks me.

I pull my hand away from the wall. "Yeah. Sorry, I was just spacing off."

He gives me a worried smile, but focuses on the task at hand and keeps walking until we reach the end of the hallway where there's another door.

"I wonder what's on the other side." I say.

"A spare bedroom," Aleesa says, gazing up at the ceiling.

Laylen presses his ear to the door. "I don't hear anything…" He grips the doorknob and turns it. "Get ready," he says, then pushes it open.

It's a bedroom with a bedframe and a dusty dresser. And chained to one of the stones wall is my mom. She just escaped from being a prisoner a few days ago and it tears at my heart to see her like this. She looks like she's sleeping, her head slumped over, her shoulders hunched. There is a piece of duct-tape over her mouth and I run up to her and carefully pull it off.

"Mom," I say, hooking a finger under her chin and tipping her head up. "Can you hear me?"

Her head bobs as she blinks at me, tears staining her cheeks. "Gemma," she croaks. "Is that you?"

"It's okay." I reach for the chain around her wrist. "We're going to get you out of here."

She blinks again dazedly and then starts to panic. "You have to go. You have to go now." She tugs at the chains, causing the skin on her wrist to split open and bleed. "It's a trap. Gemma, go! GO!"

A chill slithers down my spine as I turn around and see a thick fog crawling across the floor. Ice covers across the walls, the ceiling, and the floor in a split second and the temperature rapidly drops.

"Can you get the chains off her?" I ask Laylen.

He takes hold of one of the chains and bends the links, trying to get the heavy metal to snap apart. But it's thick and covered with the Death Walker's ice.

"Give me just a minute," he says as he continues to try to get the metal to break.

Aleesa lets out a high-pitched scream, covers her ears, and backs into the corner of the room. "Help me!"

I hear the sound of heavy footsteps heading in our direction, one by one. I glance back at Laylen, still struggling to get the chains undone.

"I'm hurrying," he says, jerking on the chains. "The damn things are thick and the ice is making it worse."

I face the doorway, where the fog is blowing in. This strange calm settles over me and I block everything out as a power takes over my body and mind, one stronger than I've ever felt, like every part of my brain is in tune with my body. Suddenly, I know what I have to do to protect us and the strange thing is I know that I can.

I raise the Sword of Immortality in front of me, the tip aimed at the door. My heart rate slows, steadies, my nerves dissipate. When the first Death Walker enters the room, cloaked and eyes glowing, I swing the sword at it and without missing a beat, stab the blade into its heart. Its yellow eyes fire up as its body drops lifelessly to the floor.

I don't have time to prepare myself as another one comes barreling. I do a twirl and then the sword jabs into the Death Walker's heart, again without any mishaps. I do this again and again, the sword sinking through each of their rotting chests. The bodies are piling up as I move like a pro, swinging the sword gracefully, my feet moving harmoniously with it.

But more keep coming and before I know it, the room is filled with Death Walkers. The stench of death is in the air as they circle me, blowing their Chill of Death in my direction but I manage to duck out of the way every time.

Then the crowd parts and Stephan comes walking in, wearing a black cloak. He gazes at the Death Walkers' bodies all over the floor and then at me. "Well, I see that you've changed since the last time I met you," he says, sounding both annoyed and impressed. He stalks toward me, his boots cracking the icy floors.

I remain where I am, waiting until he's within sword's reach before I take a stab at him. But he swats the sword away as if my new inner strength is nothing but a minor problem, insignificant.

"You know, you're a very hard girl to track down," he says. "I send a faerie to find you, but he up and disappears. I'd try to find you myself, track you down and come where you are, but that's impossible right now thanks to the *memoria extracto*."

It's like he's about to give me the same speech again, like he did in the Wastelands, which has me wondering if he's oblivious to the fact that he's captured me once before, branded me with the mark, and tried to get me to murder Alex.

"Finally, I thought to myself, what can I do?" he continues on unknowingly. "How can I get ahold of my star without going to her?" He takes the knife he's holding and traces the tip along the scar on his cheek, circling around me. "See, the thing is, Gemma, there's something you don't understand." He gives a dramatic pause and then grins. "I always win."

Yep, stuck on repeat. I check behind me, relieved to find that Laylen has freed my mother from the chains. Aleesa is still curled in the corner, rocking back and forth as she hugs her knees to her chest. I need to get us out of here. Somehow.

"I wouldn't put so much trust in people." Stephan says. "You never know what secrets they could be hiding from you. People are great liars, especially when it comes to protecting themselves."

"And you would be the expert on that, wouldn't you?" I carry his intimidating gaze with confidence.

He stops in front of me. "I'm not the only one in this room who is an expert at lying." He looks behind me at my mother on the floor her eyes unexpectedly vacant of emotion. "Should I tell her? Or would you like to, Jocelyn?"

She says nothing and Laylen shifts his weight uneasily. I discretely point at Aleesa, mouthing for Laylen to get a hold of her and get closer to me. I need to foresee us out of here. Now.

"Ask her what's on her wrist," Stephan says to me with a wicked grin. "Go ahead. Ask your mother what she's been hiding from you"

I don't have to look. I think deep down I already know. "No... there's no way," I say in denial.

Laylen bends over and jerks up the sleeve of my mother's shirt. His eyes widen and I gasp at the triangle outlining by red symbol branded in her flesh on her arm.

I shake my head, refusing to believe what's right in front of me. "It's not real..."

"She's had it forever," Stephan tells me, pleased. "Sophia, Marco... Didn't you ever wonder how I got everyone to do what I asked? The only ones I didn't mark were the ones who couldn't be marked." He frowns. "The one's whose blood is pure from evil."

I think about Alex. Aislin. Laylen. Myself. Blood pure from evil. I know I can be marked, but what about them. What if one of them is marked?

I start to step back toward the door, needing to get the hell out of here.

Stephan matches my step, regaining every amount of space I put between us. "Your mother's a fighter. She was always a fighter... it's her gift, you know—her Keeper's gift. She always made things difficult for me, which is part of the reason why I sent her to The Underworld. I couldn't even summon her to go—I had to threaten your wellbeing. The Underworld has weakened her, though. It's tainted her blood, which makes things less complicated for me. Getting her to come here was as easy as a master whistling to call his dog." He looks over at my mother, pride beaming as if she's something he's created. "It makes her easier to control. All I had to do was tug at the leash a little."

"Okay, this conversation is getting a little too metaphorical for me," I say glancing at Laylen who has Aleesa now and my mother by his side. "If you want to say something," I tell Stephan. "Just say it. Quit rambling."

He begins rolling up the sleeves of his shirt, still grinning. A small part of me wants to see how this fight will turn out, especially with my new badass fighting skills. But the other part of me knows what needs to be done. So with one swift dive, I slide across the icy floor, slipping between the Death Walkers' legs and into my mom like a baseball player glides into home plate. I snatch hold of Laylen's arm who grabs onto Aleesa and then extend a hand out to my mom. Even though she's imprinted with evil, I'm not leaving her behind.

Stephan's elation plummets as he sees his precious star slipping through his fingers like sand. "Get her!" he orders to the Death Walkers and they begin to close in on us, sucking away any heat left in the air.

But I blink my eyes and picture somewhere safe and moments later we're gone.

Chapter 16

Alex and Aislin are drinking coffee and having a heated conversation about something when the four of us fall into the living room, a pile of tangled bodies. We end up taking out the coffee table, breaking two of the legs off and cracking the top in half. Coffee spills all over the floor and Aislin gasps in alarm.

I immediately unwind my legs and arms from Laylen and Aleesa and scramble to my feet. "We have to leave," I say. "Now." I bend down to eye level with my mom who is disoriented. "Did you tell him where we were hiding?"

She trembles, pulling her knees against her chest. "I'm so sorry, Gemma. I wanted to tell you, but I couldn't."

I didn't want apologies right now. I need to know if we are safe. "I need to know if you told Stephan where we were hiding."

She didn't answer, because she couldn't.

"Shit." I start to turn to Alex for help but feel an unfamiliar sense of leadership taking control of me, coiling through my veins and colliding into my heart, thrusting a surge of energy potently through my body. "We need to leave now."

"What the fuck is going on?" Alex rounds the broken table toward me and looks at Aleesa, cowering near the end table with her arms cradled around her head. "And who the hell is she?"

"She's just someone we found in the basement." I know that once I say who she is, it's going to be a huge distraction. And we need to focus on getting somewhere safe first. "It's not important right now."

He questions me with a crook of his brow. "Okay, well then explain why we need to leave in such a rush?"

I snatch hold my mom's arm, roll her sleeve back, and give an exaggerated gesture at the mark on her wrist. "Because of that."

His jaw nearly hits the floor. "What the... did he just do that to her?"

I shake my head, letting go of her arm and my mom hangs her head in shame. "But I'll explain everything later, okay? I think she told him where we were hiding so we need to move before he shows up here... well, when he can. I'm not sure how long he still has to stay away from us, but I don't want to take any chances."

He starts ripping the place apart, pulling out weapons he hid all over the house. "Alright, everyone, we're going. Aislin, grab whatever you need to, but no clothes or stupid shit like that."

"Any suggestions on where we should go?" I collect the mapping ball from the coffee table.

"I'm running out of ideas," Alex replies, tucking a dagger into a sheath on his ankle. "With all the moving around we've been doing, the list of safe places is dwindling."

I can't believe I'm about to say this. "What if we went back to Wyoming?" I ask. "Back to Marco and Sophia's home, because I'm guessing my landlord has evicted me by now from my apartment."

"Gemma, Stephan knows where that is," Aislin tells me, like I am an idiot as she tosses herbs and candles into a large duffel bag.

"Yeah, which means he's less likely to look for us there." I pace back and forth. "He would never think we'd go to a place he knew about, right? And I'm familiar with it and the town. There are hardly any people around so it makes the worry of someone seeing us low."

"And what if Marco and Sophia are there?" Aislin asks, zipping up the bag. "Then what?"

"Then we take them out." Alex draws a medium size knife out from the sofa cushion and touches the tip of it with his finger. "We lock them up and see if we can get some answers from them. We should have done that a long time ago anyway."

Aislin sighs, but doesn't protest. Laylen comes hurrying out from the bedroom with a bag on his back. "So what's the plan?" He directs the question to me.

"Afton," I reply with confidence.

"Look at you," Laylen jokes as he adjusts the handle of the bag on his shoulder. "First the ninja moves and now the awesome leadership skills. You're turning into a regular badass."

Alex elevates his eyebrows inquisitively. "Ninja moves?"

"I'll explain later," I say dismissively. "Now what's the best way to get there? Transport or should I use my power?"

"Either." Alex goes over to the window and peers out of the blinds. "Driving isn't an option since the car was totaled in the accident."

"That's too many for me to transport all at once." Aislin hitches the bag over her shoulder. "But I can make two trips."

"No!" Alex and I shout at the same time and Aislin flinches.

"Sorry," Alex says with limited sincerity in his tone. "But remember what happened the last time we did that? You and Laylen never made it there."

"Yeah, I remember." Aislin shudders.

"It's okay...I can do it." I hope the extra adrenaline pumping through my veins will give me the boost I need to do this right.

"Are you sure?" Alex asks restlessly as he makes his way back over to me. "I don't want you over exerting yourself. You've already been passing out a lot."

"I'll be okay." And for once, it actually feels like the truth. This unknown power pumping inside me makes me feel almost invincible.

We all gather in the corner, in a tight huddle and then I close my eyes, picturing the high ridged mountains enclosing the town I grew up in, the red brick house, the rooms inside. When I open my eyes, I cringe. All six of us are huddled together in the center of my old living room. There are pictures on the walls that don't include me and sad memories are floating everywhere like ghosts. I stand up straight, a mixture of feelings drowning me. Everything... It's too much.

My eyes roll into the back of my head and I buckle to the floor.

Chapter 17

When I wake up in my old bed, I flip out. For the briefest, most fearful moment I think that maybe I've dreamt the last year and have woken up to my lonely high school life, friendless, unfeeling and empty once again.

Everything looks exactly the same as the last time I was here, back a couple of months ago. The walls are bright red and there's a single shelf in the corner that use to hold my limited collection of books and CDs but Sophia made me come get them because she didn't want my "junk" taking up her space any-more. The only thing that is different is the six-foot-four vampire snoring away in my computer chair, his black boots kicked up on the computer desk, his head tipped back in an awkward position.

I find myself smiling as I get out of bed and pad over to him. I don't try to wake him right away, taking in his pale skin, the silver lip ring ornamenting his bot-tom lip, and the mark of immortality on his arm. God, he is beautiful. He really is and honestly, I don't think he sees the beauty in himself, inside and out, which is sad.

Jessica Sorensen

I lightly tap him on the shoulder, figuring I'll wake him up and see what's going on. He jumps, startled, and lets out a loud snort, his fangs descending from his mouth as if he's about to bite.

"Sorry." I cover my mouth to stifle a laugh. "I didn't mean to scare you."

His bright blue eyes are huge as he presses his hand to his heart. "You scared the shit out of me. Jesus, Gemma." He allows his fangs to retract as he lowers his feet to the floor.

"Sorry." I lower my hand from my mouth. "But why are you sleeping at my computer desk?"

"I'm on Gemma duty."

"Gemma duty?"

"Yeah, Gemma duty." Laylen fiddles with his lip ring, sucking it between his teeth. "You've been out for almost three days and we were getting worried about you...that maybe the *rush* was too much for you. You're heart's been racing way too fast so they put me in here to try to calm you."

"With your gift?" I ask and he nods and it makes my stomach flutter just a bit. "Wait. What's a *rush*?"

Laylen swivels in the chair. "It's the rush of adrenaline you get when your Keeper's mark first appears."

My arms go limp at my side. "My Keeper's mark?"

174

He offers me a smile but it doesn't quite reach his eyes. "Yeah it's on your shoulder blade."

I dash over to the mirror and yank down the upper part of my t-shirt, turning around. Circling the center of my shoulder blade is a ring of fiery-gold flames, centered by a circle. "Wait." I give him a suspicious glance. "How did you guys find the mark on me?"

He gave me a devious smile, waggling his eyebrows. "How do you think?"

I pick up a pillow off my bed and throw it at him, even though I wouldn't really mind if he had looked. I trust him enough.

He catches the pillow effortlessly. "I'm joking. We just checked the obvious places—the arms, the ankles, your shoulders. If we wouldn't have been able to find it, we would have waited for you to wake up and let you check the rest of your body."

I touch the mark on my shoulder. "God, I can't believe I'm a Keeper... I didn't even think it could happen to me."

"You didn't think those awesome fighting moves came from nowhere, did you?" Laylen says, cocking an eyebrow at me.

"So, you knew what was going on back at the castle?"

175

"I assumed as much."

"You seem in a good mood," I say, picking up a CD from the desk and absentmindedly turn it around in my hand, something Sophia forgot to pack up.

He shrugs. "It's weird, but as soon as you got your mark, your blood stopped being like a drug to me."

"So you don't crave blood anymore?" I wonder. "All because I got the mark."

"Well I still crave blood," he says, standing up. "And yours still smells extra mouthwatering, but it's not as mind consuming as it was."

"Is it normal for you not to crave a Keepers blood as much?"

He nods. "Yeah, it's one of their many defense mechanisms."

I set the CD case down. "So you're happy I'm one then?"

His happiness diminishes. "I never said that." He scratches the back of his neck. "Honestly, I was kind of hoping it'd skip over you. But not because I don't like you now… I just really liked you before and some-times getting the mark changes people."

"I still feel like the same person," I tell him. "Just stronger."

He smiles again, nudging my foot with his. "I'm sure you'll stay the clumsy, emotional, caring Gemma I first met."

"I hope so." And I really do, but I can't help but think of Stephan and wonder what he was like before he got his Keeper mark. Perhaps he was once good, too. "So what's been going on for the last few days while I was out?" I ask, changing the subject.

"Not much." He tucks his hands into the pockets of his jeans as he sits down on the edge of my bed. "In fact, it's been pretty quiet."

"What about my mom?" I ask, taking a seat beside him. "How's she doing?"

He hesitates, plucking a loose string on one of the throw pillows. "Everyone thought it would be best, including her, if we locked her up until we can figure out what to do with her. We don't want her sneaking off and doing something like what she just did."

"It wasn't her fault. It's the mark's fault. She can't help what she does. Trust me, I know what it feels like." I touch the spot on my arm where the mark once was. "Even though I erased the vision, I can still feel what I felt like while I was possessed."

Laylen sets the pillow aside. "I know it's not her fault, but we have to be careful. And Aislin's trying to figure out a spell to remove the mark," he says. "She's been searching the internet like crazy for the last few days, but no luck yet. The problem is we don't know who we can trust to go to for information. She can't just go walking into a witch store and ask how to remove the Mark of Malefiscus. Aislin also went pretty spell crazy; she put like a ton of spells all over the house, trying to keep us protected from unannounced visitors. And thankfully there are no signs that Marco and Sophia have been here in a while. The mail and newspapers are piling up. Aislin tried to do a Tracker Spell and either they have a protection charm on them or… or they've died because they're not showing up anywhere."

"Died?" I'm not sure how I feel about that.

He sighs and comes over to me. "Are you going to be okay?"

I shrug. "I'm not sure, I think so, but…" The prickle is erratic on the back of my neck, but I don't know what it's telling me. To be sad? If it's that, it's not working because I just feel numb. All those years of living with them, but being practically invisible, the emotional bond never formed and now I can barely remember them at all.

"What's wrong?" He puts a finger under my chin and angles my head up so I'm looking at him.

"It's just that it's so weird to be in here again," I say, glancing around the bare room. "Nothing about this room feels like me, yet it's the room I grew up in."

He takes in the bareness of my room. "Maybe that's because this room isn't you. I mean, all those years you spent living here you weren't really you." He gives me a hug and then we leave the room and go downstairs. On our way down, he tells me how Aleesa is recovering and that Alex and Aislin seem to be reacting to her okay.

"What about marks?" I ask. "Does she have any on her?"

"You mean, the Mark of Malefiscus?" he checks.

I nod. "Stephan said he'd been putting it on everyone who didn't have pure blood." I bite my lip, hating myself for wondering if Aislin, Alex, and even Laylen have one.

"Aislin came up with a spell for that too." He takes my hand in his. "Come on and I'll have her show you."

In the living room, Aislin is sitting cross-legged on the floor squinting at a computer screen that's on the coffee table in front of her. Alex is on the sofa, watching TV with his feet kicked up and a glass in his hand that's filled with a golden liquid, probably tequila or something similar. It's weird to see because... well, because everything appears so ordinary and it feels so unnatural.

But then I notice Aislin is searching the web for mark removal spells, and Alex is also sharpening a sword and everything feels right in the world again.

"Oh, thank God," Aislin says, relaxing when she sees me. "I thought you weren't going to wake up."

"You guys always think that," I say, letting go of Laylen's hand when I notice her gaze drifting to it. "Yet I always do." There's a lightness in my tone, one I've never heard before.

Aislin clicks the computer mouse. "You seem in a good mood." There's speculation in her voice as if she's wondering what Laylen and I were up to before we came down here.

"It's because of the lingering adrenaline from the *rush*." Alex eyes leisurely travel up my legs, across my midsection and chest, and ultimately land on my eyes.

God, he's so intense that I want to lean down, run my hands through his messy hair while I feel the soft- ness of his lips against mine. I'm not sure how long we stare at each other like that, but eventually Laylen clears his throat, something I'm realizing he has to do a lot when Alex and I are near each other.

"What's our next move?" Laylen sits down and I follow, tucking my legs under my ass. Alex remains staring at me with way too much heat in his eyes. If he keeps it up, I'm going to drop dead right here on the sofa in front of everyone.

"Has anyone talked to my mother yet?" I ask. "Or is it pointless because of the mark?"

"We made the same Blood Promise with her as we did with Nicholas, then we got some information out of her." Alex lifts his hand, showing me a healing cut on his palm.

"What did she tell you?" I ask. "Did she say how she ended up at the Keeper's Castle?"

Alex grows grave. "*He* called her," he says tightly. "As in he *summoned* her there by the mark. Apparently, Stephan can summon people with the Mark of Malefiscus."

I can't help but think of the mark again, hidden on her flesh out of sight. "How do we know he's not going to summon her right now?"

"We don't," Alex says straightforwardly, putting the sword he was sharpening down on the coffee table. "But we've got her locked up and we took away her Key of Malefiscus so that might help."

My mouth curves downward into a frown. "Great. He has his own key now."

"He's had one all along apparently," Alex explains bitterly. "I guess as he marked each one of the Keepers with the Mark of Malefiscus, he also gave them a key, so when he touches his mark, they can take the key, trace a door wherever they are and it takes them straight to the castle."

"So Nicholas had one of those too, I'm guessing. And Marco and Sophia?" I say in astonishment.

"Nicholas didn't have one, I don't think," Alex says. "Jocelyn said that Stephan gave them only to the Keepers he marked."

"Do any of you have one?" I don't want to say it but I need to know.

"Oh yeah," Laylen says, shifting his legs out in front of them to stretch. "Aislin, show Gemma the spell you came up with to know when people nearby have the mark."

Aislin's eyes light up as she pops her knuckles. "All right, Gemma, here goes nothing."

***

About a half of an hour later, I'm convinced none of them have marks. Aislin does a spell that shows my mother's mark and lights it up, then does it on the rest of them including Aleesa, and it shows all three of them are mark free. She also does it on me, so they'll know that I'm free of evil at the moment. Then I go upstairs to talk with my mom in private because it seems like we have a lot to talk about.

Sophia's room is the same, white linens, walls, and curtains. Everything is clean and tidy, the bed made, clothes tucked away.

My mom looks miserable lying on the floor, bound to the wall by chains fastened to her wrists. Her head is resting on a pillow, her brown hair a halo around her head, and her eyes are shut as if she's sleeping.

I close the door behind me and her eyes open as she sits up. "Sorry, I didn't mean to wake you up," I say, lingering near the doorway. Finally I dare to sit in front of her, leaving just enough room so that she can't reach me with the chains, just in case. "I don't know what to say," I tell her honestly, fidgeting with the leather band on my wrist.

"I'm sorry, Gemma," she says, although there's emptiness in her eyes, reminding me that deep down this isn't my mother.

"It's okay. I get that you couldn't say anything about the mark." I pause. "But there's one thing I don't understand.... How is it that you're marked and yet you could tell us all those things that day—about the ending of the world? And Stephen's plan?"

"There are always loopholes, Gemma."

"You keep saying that, but it doesn't make sense to me yet."

"I know. Some things are hard to understand and even harder to explain." She scoots back and rests her head against the wall. "Sometimes my mind gets cloudy as if it doesn't belong to me, and I say words that aren't my own but it's not cloudy right now, because of the Blood Promise. But that won't last forever... I won't last forever."

Panic claws up my throat. "You're not leaving me again, are you?"

She doesn't answer right away. "Remember how you told me that you saw the vision of Stephan forcing me into the lake? Well, you don't understand the vision completely. There were things that happened that confused you. Stephan didn't force me into the lake, like he—you—thought," she says quietly, almost remorseful. "I went in there on my own... I chose to go to The Underworld on my own."

I pull my legs up and rest my chin on my knee. "No you didn't... I saw him force you to go in there."

She crawls toward me, reaching for my hand, dragging the chains across the floor with her. "No, you didn't. That's what it may have looked like, but that's not what happened," she says, frowning when I slide back out of her reach. "I've always had this gift... kind of like super willpower, and for the longest time, even after Stephan marked me, it stayed with me—made me strong against his attempted tries at making me evil."

"When did he mark you? Didn't you fight back?"

"That's hard to do when there are Death Walkers. He created his army of death and picked us off one by one. Some didn't make it out alive like Laylen's parents."

"I—I—But he told me his parents died in a car accident right after you were sent to The Underworld?"

"No, they died putting up a fight when Stephan ambushed them."

A massive lump lodges in my throat. "Does Laylen know this?"

She shakes her head, kneeling in front of me. "There is a lot of memory tampering that's gone on throughout the years, including with Laylen."

I remember Laylen mentioning memory loss once, when he was turned into a vampire. "But then why did you choose to go to The Underworld?" I ask, fearing her answer. "Why would you ever *want* to go to a place like that? So full of death and torture?"

"Because I could feel Stephan gaining control over me," she whispers, her eyes wide as she gazes off. "I was the hardest to gain control over. Even after he marked me, he still couldn't get me to do the things he wanted, especially when it came to you. But he kept working and breaking me down and finally I felt my willpower diminishing. I knew it wouldn't be long before I wouldn't have power over my actions and I just couldn't do it—I couldn't stand around and watch them detach your soul and ruin your life."

"So you decided just to leave me then?" I'm trying very hard not to get angry, but it's difficult and I can feel aggravation simmering under my skin. "Even though you knew they would still take away my soul?"

"I'm so sorry." She reaches for me again, her blue irises begging for me to understand. "But even if I stayed, it would have happened still."

So my mom never sacrificed her life to try and save mine. She sacrificed it so she wouldn't have to watch my life get ruined. That was the real reason and it hurt, like a knife lodged in my heart.

"So you wish I never went and saved you from The Underworld?" My anger rises through my voice as I scoot away from her.

She shakes her head erratically. "*No*. I understand now that running away doesn't solve anything. Everything still happened to you, and instead of trying to fight, I gave up. I'll never give up again. We'll figure out a way to fix this."

"And how are we supposed to fix it?" I snap. "Do you know how to work a fucking mapping ball? Because I sure as hell don't."

"Alex told me about that." Her eyes flash cold. "So you saw your father?"

"Yeah, I saw him. And thanks for telling me he's still alive."

"Did he tell you what he did?" she asks harshly. "Did he tell you how he ended the world?"

"He said he made some mistakes and changed and recreated a vision so the world would end," I tell her. "But he didn't explain why."

"He changed the vision because he wanted one of these." She shoves up the sleeve of her shirt and extends her arm out, showing me the Mark of Malefiscus on her wrist just below the cuff on the chain.

I recoil away from her, shaking my head "No, I don't believe you."

She carries my gaze steadily. "Yes, he did. He wanted the mark. He wanted it."

"Why!?" I cry, tears stinging the corners of my eyes.

"For power—he wanted to be powerful, just like Stephan."

I leap to my feet, trembling with rage, fists clenched, adrenalin soaring so violently I feel like I'm getting whiplash. "You're lying. He wouldn't be trying to fix it, if that's the truth." My feelings don't match my words, though. I've wondered this myself. But what she's saying is making me furious for some reason, perhaps because she's confirming what everyone else has been worried about—that my father is evil.

"Time changes people's minds." She tries to get to her feet, but the weight of the chains drags her back to the floor. "And he's been locked up alone in the Room of Forbidden for so long, I'm sure he's had time to clear all the hunger for power out of his head."

"No, you're lying!" I shout. "My father didn't make this mess because he wanted to be powerful like Stephan, because he wanted the Mark of Malefiscus. There's no way." But a voice whispers in my head, telling me maybe she's right.

"You barely know him," she says sadly. "You have no idea what he would or wouldn't do."

I storm out of the room, slamming the door shut behind me. My mother calls out my name, but I hurry down the hall and burst into my room. All that time invested in wondering about my parents, only to find out that one wants to be evil and one is imprinted with evil.

I snatch a brush off my dresser and chuck it across the room. It makes a loud thump as it dents the wall, and bits and pieces of paint and drywall crumble to the floor. Then I slump to the ground and lean back against the door. What am I supposed to do? Try to get back to where my dad is—to the Room of Forbidden—and get some more details on how to fix his mistakes? I'm not sure I want to do that. Not after what I was just told.

"What am I going to do?" I whisper.

Just then, the sunlight hits my window and filters through my room, onto my bed and rays of maroon reflect across my walls and ceiling. I get to my feet and inch toward my bed cautiously and see a small crystal ball filled with rubies on one of my pillows. I look around my room for someone but it's empty. With an unsteady hand, I pick up the crystal and discover a piece of paper tucked beneath it.

"Go to the City of Crystal and get the Purple Flame. Sincerely, a friend," I read aloud.

I flip the paper over, but there's nothing on the back. I go over to the window, push it open, and look down at the driveway and I catch a hint of a flowery scent. But it's probably just my imagination.

Chapter 18

"The Purple Flame?" Aislin pulls a face at the paper. She's still sitting on the floor of the living room with the laptop opened up on the coffee table and the note I found in my room in her hand. "I think it's a Foreseer term."

"Does anyone know what it is?" I take the note from her hand and read it over again, pondering whose handwriting it could be.

"No," Alex says, absentmindedly playing with my hair as he sits next to me, mulling it over. "We're all just as lost as you."

"Well, does anyone know how to find out what it is?" I ask, knowing I should go sit somewhere else, but I can't seem to will myself to give up the comfort he's instilling in me. And after the thing with my mom, I really need some comfort. "Is there a book or something? Or can we search it out on the Internet?"

Alex and Aislin exchange a look of inquiry. "What do you think?" Alex asks her. "Would it say anything about it?"

"I don't know…maybe," Aislin deliberates as she clicks a few keys on the computer and then shuts it down. "But it would be extremely risky, especially if he's at our house."

My eyes blink incredulously. "You want to go to your house—to Stephan's house?"

"Maybe. I mean he has a book." Aislin scoots the laptop to the side and crosses her arms on the table.

"A history book," Alex adds. "That outlines the history of the Foreseers. And it's probably our best bet on figuring this out since we don't have a Foreseer around to help us anymore."

My stomach churns as I think of Nicholas and the floral scent I detected only moments ago when I looked outside my window. But there's no way... Nicholas is dead.

"I'll go get it," Alex announces, getting up to head to the foyer. "My father was never home anyway, so I doubt he'll be hanging around now, but if he is, I can handle it."

I want to grab him and refuse to let him go, but deep down I know someone has to do it and I've already talked him into letting me do things by myself once before, when I was going to the castle, and since it didn't turn out so great, I know convincing him of such a thing again would be even more difficult. "At least let me foresee us there."

He shakes his head, lingering in the doorway. "You can't. There's *Praesidium* everywhere in the yard and basement, and besides, you don't know what my place looks like."

I motion at Aislin. "Well, let her transport you ..."

"No one can use magic in the house," he explains, leaning against the doorframe with his arms folded.

"Why?"

He shrugs. "Since we knew about all the things that go bump in the night, we wanted to be protected."

"So you're just going to drive there?" It seems like such a normal thing to do which makes it seem odd.

"Basically, yeah. But don't worry, I'll be okay," he promises. "There's like a one percent chance he'll be there. He was never even there while we were growing up—he never was anywhere we were unless it was convenient for him."

"Can you at least wait until dark, so he doesn't see you coming if he's there? Plus, there'll be lights on in the house if someone's home so you'll know," I point out, walking toward him.

He winks at me. "Alright, but only because you asked me to."

Unsure how to respond to his composed demeanor, I smile tightly. But it feels wrong because I'm afraid. Afraid of getting hurt. Of not being able to fix the world's outcome. And the scariest one of all, losing him.

***

For the rest of the day, we keep to ourselves, getting lost in our own worry. Aleesa comes downstairs eventually, looking better than when I first met her. Her tangles are tamed, her skin isn't so pale, and she has on clean clothes. Aislin takes her into the kitchen to feed her. She's almost like a child, unable to take care of herself and I feel sorry for her, realizing that there are so many people's lives that have been ruined by Stephan and I wonder how many more there are.

I'm sitting on the couch, trying to watch the television and not think about all the danger I'm faced with, but all I can do is focus on Alex and think about how I don't want him to go. He seems content, however, humming a song under his breath as he laces his boots.

"I don't think you should go alone," I finally say, turning off the television. "I should go with you. I'm a Keeper now, so I'm not completely useless."

He puts a knife into the pocket of his jeans and rolls up the sleeves of his long-sleeve shirt, giving me a good glimpse of his lean muscles. "No way."

"You didn't see me at the castle." I position myself in front of him as he's walking out of the room. "I kicked some major Death Walker ass."

He eyes me over from head to toe. "You know what, you can go if you want. You're a Keeper now, and this will be good practice for you. You can be my lookout, even though I'm sure my father won't show up. But better safe than sorry, right? And besides, I want you near me at all times. I'm not sure I'll have a clear head if you're not there."

"You're always saying that," I tell him, fighting the urge to kiss him. It's been almost four days since I was graced with his mouth and being this close to him is causing the sparks to attack me and make me want to attack him.

"That's because it's true." He reaches out to touch me, but pulls away. I've been noticing how much easier it is for him not to touch me. Ever since the mark showed up, he seems to have regained some control over his emotions. Maybe they've fizzled or something.

The sparks however, have not. I can feel them dancing across my skin, taunting me. "Is there something wrong?"

"Why would there be something wrong?"

"I don't know..." I feel embarrassed to ask him if he's lost interest in me and even more embarrassed that it's so important to me. "Nothing. Never mind."

"Gemma, just say it. You don't need to sensor yourself with me."

"Are you about ready to go?" Aislin announces as she enters the room, stopping our conversation, probably for the better. "Because it's getting late."

"Gemma's going with me." Alex picks up a slender sword from off the table, tosses it to me, and I surprisingly catch it effortlessly.

"I don't think that's such a good idea," Aislin protests. "In fact, I think it's a really stupid idea."

"We'll be fine," Alex assures her. "I really don't think Stephan will be there."

Aislin shakes her head. "That's not what I'm worried about. I don't think he'll be there either." She pauses, glancing back and forth between us. "What I'm worried about is you two being alone together in an empty house ... you've already been pushing the boundaries and I'm worried you're going to end up killing each other here soon."

"Wow. Way to put it out there," I say sarcastically.

"Sorry," she tells me unapologetically. "But I have to be blunt because it's serious stuff, you know."

"We'll be fine." Alex rolls his eyes and again I wonder if something has changed between us since he seems so convinced he'll be able to stay away from me. "We won't do anything we wouldn't do here." He presses back a smile as he pretends to examine the sword.

Aislin sighs. "Fine, but please hurry."

We nod and then head out the door.

***

For most of the drive, we're quiet, the sparks heating the longer we're in trapped in the confinements of the car, but they only seem to bother me. Alex seems fully comfortable being in the car with me, driving down the road with the music blasting. Eventually he turns down a side road that goes up into the foothills of the mountains. Not too far up the road, he makes a sudden veer to the left, dipping my old Mazda I used to drive to school into the trees and bushes.

I press my hand to the dashboard, bracing myself against the bumps. "What are you doing?"

197

He kills the headlights as he slows the car to a stop and everything around us gets taken out by night. "I didn't want to pull up the driveway, just in case someone is there."

"You know this doesn't have four-wheel drive, right?"

"It made it, didn't it?" There's humor in his voice.

I don't say anything further as we get out of the car and hike up the dirt hill. I can barely see anything around me and wish that Aislin's night vision spell was a permanent thing. But I notice that I do a lot less stumbling than I used to, probably because I'm a Keeper now.

When we approach the top of the hill, Alex hunkers down behind a bush, and puts his arm in front of me, signaling for me to stay behind him as he assesses the situation.

"I knew no one would be here," he mutters after getting a good look at the dark house in the distance. He stands back up and steps out of the trees and onto a gravel path that leads to a three-story home, but that's about all I can see. At the front door, he takes a key from under a glass mushroom and unlocks the door.

As I stepped inside the foyer, he retrieves a flashlight out of his back pocket and beams the light around. "It stinks in here," he murmurs, fanning his hand in front of his face. "Like feet."

I plug my nose. "And like someone forgot to take out the garbage, but I'm guessing that's a good sign that no one's been here in a while."

He nods. "Welcome to my home," he mutters under his breath as he starts for the spiral staircase in front of us.

We climb up the stairs and go into a room with black and purple walls, dark blue carpet, and a massive canopy bed decorated with vines and curtains.

"Whose room is this?" I take in the posters on the wall, the decorations, the clutter, signs that someone actually had a life in here and it makes me a bit sad.

He sweeps the flashlight around to room. "It's Aislin's."

I'm so confused. "But it's so... so... awesome. And not frilly and pink."

He opens the closet door. "You have to understand something about Aislin. She's not who she appears to be on the outside. She has a darker side to her." He sets the flashlight down on the floor, aiming it up at the ceiling, and then grabs a box from the top shelf. "Most witches do have a darker side...but my father trained her to be the girl she is on the outside so people wouldn't see her as a threat." He peers inside the box and then puts it away. "He controlled her a lot."

He starts rummaging around in the closet while I wander around the room. I see a photo on top of the dresser of Aislin and Laylen, sitting on a porch swing, smiling and happy, something that doesn't exist at the moment and my heart knots in my chest.

"What are you looking for?" I go back into the closet and move up behind Alex.

He yanks a box decorated with black and purple glitter off the top closet shelf and lifts the lid. "For this." Inside the box, are bags of herbs, a collection of candles and crystals, beads, necklaces, and other strange items that have to be Wicca stuff.

"Aislin's spell stuff?" I pick up a necklace with a rose pendant.

"Yeah, I figured we could pick it up while we were here," he says.

I put the necklace back in the box. "It's a good idea. We have been using her magic a lot."

He nods, then we leave Aislin's room with the box, crossing the hallway into an office area with shelves for walls that are crammed with old books, a large desk in the corner, and antique furniture.

"Please tell me you know where the Foreseer book is," I say in a hopeful expression.

He shakes his head, crushing my hope into a thousand pieces. So we start looking, working our way from bottom to top, until we're up to our elbows in books. Alex has the flashlight between us, so there was just enough light that we can see the titles on the covers.

"I love books," I admit when the silence between us starts to make me restless.

"I know," he says, peeking inside a book.

"How?"

"Because you loved them when you were younger." He quickly clears his throat as if he's said something wrong.

"What else did I like when I was younger?" I ask, adding the book in my hand to the stack beside me.

His eyes travel from the book to me. "You drove me crazy sometimes." There's a sparkle in his eyes.

I roll my eyes. "I did not."

He nods with certainty, putting the book on top of a stack and then collecting another one. "You were always such a daredevil and it drove me nuts keeping you out of trouble."

"Then why did you?" I crisscross my legs.

"Because I wanted to." He looks down at the book as he reads the spine then the front.

"What about you?" I ask. "What were you like?"

It takes him longer to respond. "An asshole."

"I'm sure you weren't always an asshole." I give him a playful smile and he shakes his head, stifling a grin.

"I don't know, Gemma," he says, exhaling loudly. "I had a rough childhood, full of shitty memories of my father doing really shitty things to me, but I don't want to talk about it with you, because it makes me more of an asshole, complaining to you about stuff like that when you suffered the most." His head tips down as he avoids eye contact with me.

"We all suffered," I say. "One way or another and I don't think you're an asshole for saying that—shit happened and we shouldn't have to keep it a secret anymore."

He glances up at me. "You sound very wise right now."

I shrug. "I was just saying how it is."

He inhales and then exhales, his gaze fastened with mine. The pull starts to arise and I find myself setting the book aside and scooting across the floor toward him. At first he stays still, as if welcoming my advance, but then he abruptly gets up and goes over to the bookshelf.

"Did I do something wrong?" I dare ask, feeling vulnerable at the moment.

He climbs up the ladder for the top shelf, shaking his head. "Why would you think that?"

"I don't know." I struggle for words I don't want to say. "You've just... you've just seemed really uninterested since I got my Keeper's mark." Feeling stupid, I engulf my attention in the book on my lap.

I hear him moving around, then moments later his boots appear in my line of vision. "That's not what it is," he says. "I'm just trying to protect you."

I look up at him. "From what?"

"From me." He sits down in front of me and there's sincerity in his eyes. "When you got the *rush* reality sort of slapped me in the face. It was so intense with you that I thought... that I thought you were going to die, which can happen sometimes. And that made me realize just how much I don't want you to die." He strokes my cheek with his finger. "I need you here and if that means keeping our distance, then that's what I'll do."

The emotion flooding his eyes is so potent, so consuming that I momentarily stop breathing. "But do you ever think…. Ever think it might be for the best," I whisper. "Because it'd put an end to all of this."

He cups my chin in his hand. "I'm not going to go there," he says forcefully, then pushes to his feet. "We'll find another way."

He goes back to searching through the book and I return to mine, but I can't help but be aware of him. So aware that even when I shut my eyes, all I see is him.

***

We don't say much to each other as we continue looking through books. It starts to get to me after a while. Surrounded by stacks, I take a look at the many left on the shelf and finally say, "What if it's not on the shelf? The book has got to be important, right, if it has the history of the Foreseers in it. Why would he keep it out in the open?" I pause remembering something from my past. "I once went looking for my birth certificate in Marco and Sophia's room."

He glances up from the book he's skimming through. "Did you find it?"

"Yeah, it was hidden in this secret compartment of this trunk they had." I point at a trunk in the corner of the room. "Kind of like that one."

Alex and I trade a curious look then we dash for the trunk, Alex swiping up the flashlight before winding around the stacks of books all over the floor. The trunk ends up being full of books and we take them out, checking the title of each one. When we reach the bottom, I push on the board, and just like the trunk at Marco and Sophia's, the bottom pops up, and there is our book. A leather bound spine and an eye on the cover; the same kind of eye on the columns at the Room of Forbidden.

"So this is it." I start to get to my feet, but Alex stays kneeling on the floor, staring into the trunk.

"What's wrong?"

He reaches inside and removes another leather book with the initials A.A. engraved on the front of it.

"Is it yours?" I tuck the Foreseer book under my arm and sit down beside him

He swallows hard as he fans through the pages. "I think it's my mother's." He looks lost as he pushes to his feet with the book in his hand. "I'm taking this with me."

Nodding, I help him pile the books back into the trunk. "Should we clean up the rest of the mess?"

Alex shakes his head, his mood off from the discovery of the book. "There's no point—"

The echo of a door slamming shut causes us to freeze.

"Shit," Alex hisses and I can feel the fear pouring off him. "Someone's here."

Chapter 19

"Do you think its Stephan?" I whisper as Alex clicks the flashlight off and night smothers us, except for a thin trail of moonlight trickling though the window.

"I'm not sure." He stuffs the flashlight into his pocket, laces his fingers through mine, the sparks crackling as he puts a finger to his lips. "Be as quiet as possible okay, no matter what happens."

We tiptoe into the hallway and turn toward the stairway, but spin around when we hear Stephan's voice drifting up the stairs, talking either on his phone or to someone else.

Alex tows me to the end of the hallway and into a room, softly shutting the door behind us. He turns the flashlight back on and scans it around. There are clothes on the floor, CD's, but the bed is unmade. The décor screams that it's a guy's room and I'm betting it's the room he grew up in.

He lets go of my hand, kicks some clothes out of the way, and then flips over a rug. Underneath it is a small trap door. He opens it and shines the light down into the small, narrow space.

"Are we both going to be able to fit?" I ask with a hint of doubt

He massages the back of his neck tensely. "We should be able to, but you get in first."

I hurry and sit down and lower myself into the hole, laying on my side and scooting as far to the side as I possibly can. Then he puts his legs in and squeezes beside me, managing to pull the rug back down as he shuts the trapdoor. He turns off the flashlight, lies on his side, facing me and I have to put my leg over his hip just so we can fit. Our bodies are pressed so tightly together that I can feel his heart pounding in his chest against mine. The electricity rapidly starts to heat up the space and within a minute were both panting. But all we can do is wait.

***

I'm not sure how much time goes by without us making or hearing a noise, but it seems like forever. The longer the stillness goes on, the more our hands start to wander all over each other's bodies. I trace my fingers up and down his back and then through his hair, while his roam up my sides, along my breasts, my hips. He keeps uttering it'll be okay, like he's touching me only to soothe me, but then they slip between my legs and he starts rubbing me.

I bite my lip hard to stifle a moan and then open my mouth to tell him not to do that because I won't be able to be quiet, but then he mutters something about this wasn't part of the plan and his lips come down roughly on mine as if he just lost a silent battle.

I kiss him back, letting his tongue delve into my mouth and then I nibble on his lip. He trades his hand for his leg, slipping his thigh up between my legs then grips my hip and encourages me to rock and rub up against him. I know it's not the time. Stephan is close and that puts our lives in danger, but it feels so goddamn good and I can't seem to find the willpower to stop.

My willpower only crumbles further when his hand slips down the front of my jeans and he slides a couple of fingers deep inside me.

I fight back a whimper and moan, murmuring, "That feels so... good."

His free hand tangles in my hair as he sucks and bites and my earlobe. "Yes... it does..." He groans himself as he continues to move his fingers inside me and I find myself putting my hand on him, rubbing him through the fabric of his jeans, moaning louder when I feel how hard he is. It's so wrong in many different ways, but as he pushes me to the edge, causing heat and blissfulness to suffocate my body and take me away, I can't think about anything else but how amazing it feels.

But moments later, I come crashing down as I hear the bedroom door open.

Alex stills beside me, and then he quickly slips his fingers out of me and puts a finger over my mouth. "Shhh...." The lust flowing off him instantly shifts to fear. I've never felt so much fear around him before and I have to wonder just how terrified he is of his father, which makes me wonder just how bad his father was to him, maybe violent.

I hold my breath and remain still. There's a soft thud followed by another, then footsteps heading across the floor. The lights turn on and then the floorboards creak. I can hear someone fumbling around, muttering under their breath. Finally the footsteps start up again. Moments later, the lights turn off and the door closes.

Neither of us budges, too afraid he's still in the room and he's trying to trick us to come out. More time goes by. An eternity. It has to be approaching morning before Alex finally speaks again.

"Stay here," he whispers in my ear. "I'll be right back."

The he climbs out of the hole while I lay inside waiting anxiously. I can hear him walking around above me, then moments later he looks back down in the hole. "It's okay. You can come up."

I get out, still carrying the Foreseer book as Alex looks around the room, then he scratches his head. "My mirror's missing." He walks up to a dresser, puzzled. "I got it from a witch who told me it would show me my future if I looked in it, but it was a bunch of shit because every time I looked in it all I saw was light."

I nearly drop the book. "You saw light?"

He nods, eyeing me suspiciously. "What's wrong?"

I shake my head. "It's nothing." It's a lie. Because it's sounds so much like the dream I keep having of us being taken away by light.

He keeps staring at me for a while, knowing I'm lying, but then gives up. "We should probably go in case he comes back," he says and then we hurry out of the house.

***

I start reading through the pages of the Foreseers' book during the drive home. The first few chapters are insignificant, but then I stumble onto something interesting.

The Room of Forbidden: A desolate place where no soul lives except the seer that committed the crime. In the Room of Forbidden, the seer will spend an eternity alone. No one can enter the Room of For-bidden, for the room exists only in the seer's mind.

The power of a Foreseer's mind: The Foreseer's mind is one of the most powerful tools. In fact, some of the more powerful Foreseers are able to push their minds to see what they need to see in times of great need.

Push the mind to see what it needs to see in times of great need? I wonder how that works because it seems like a useful thing. I flip the page, hoping for detailed instructions, but the there's only a drawing of a person with an eye on their forehead so I skim through more pages, searching for the words "purple" or "flame," but by the time Alex is parking the car in the driveway, I still haven't found anything about it.

When Alex turns off the engine, he rotates in the seat to face me. "Can we keep what happened back at the house a secret? I don't want to worry Aislin more than she already is. She's been really stressed out lately."

Nodding, I shut the book. "Of course."

"And the stuff that happened in the trapdoor." He scratches his head, looking uncomfortable. "We should probably just forget that ever happened."

The prickle stabs at the back of my neck "You want me to forget about all the times we fucked too," I say and we both wince. "Sorry," I tell him quickly. "I don't know what's coming over me."

He swiftly shakes his head. "Don't apologize. I feel the same way too." He turns away and grips the steering wheel until his knuckles turn white. "I feel so frustrated all the time... I'm usually so good at doing what I need to do... but with you... I can't seem to keep my hands off you." He takes his hands off the steering wheel and reaches for the door handle. "And I need to, to protect you."

He gets out and goes into the house. I follow moments later, pretending as if nothing happened, as if it didn't feel like my heart was breaking because there may be a chance that we never will be able to be together.

In the kitchen, Aislin is at the table with a bunch of herbs and leaves scattered in front of her, along with some candles and her spell book.

"Did you get the book?" she asks Alex as I'm locking the door.

"I've got it." I hold it up and show it to her.

Alex removes his jacket and sets it on the back of the chair, then puts the box of herbs and other magic stuff he picked up for Aislin on the table. "How's eve-rything been here?"

"Everything's been fine." She turns a page in her spell book. "Jocelyn's asleep, and Laylen's showing Aleesa what a TV is, and I'm trying to figure out a spell that will remove the mark."

I yawn, feeling exhaustion overwhelming me, not to mention the idea of being in the same room as Alex is making me feel sick. "I'm going to bed," I say then I drag myself to my bedroom, strip down into my bra and underwear, never fully making it into my pajamas as I flop down on the bed and pass out with the Fore-seer book in my hand.

Chapter 20

Light. Everywhere. I'm blinded by it, suffocating.

"It'll be all right," Alex whispers, bushing my hair out of my face. "I want to protect you forever, no matter what happens. No matter what it costs. I would die for you Gemma."

I want to tell him that I can't allow that. That if he dies, I die right along with him, not because of the star, but because of a broken heart, but my lips are sealed by an emotion surfacing, one I know I have to shove down.

The light flickers and the lake materialize before us. The water is glistening with ice, and death is in the air. They sky is grey, the clouds thick, the trees frosted with snow.

"It'll be alright," Alex says again and I clutch onto him tightly as the light drowns me. "I'm here Gemma. I'll always be here for you, no matter what."

Images flash through my mind. Death Walkers… Stephan… fire…

Then nothing but ash falling from the sky and not even Alex and I survive.

***

"Wake up. Come on, open your eyes." A hand touches my arm and there's no jolt, no spark, no warmth.

My eyes shoot open and with one swift movement I shove the person leaning over my bed down to the floor. Then I leap to my feet with my fist raised, ready to fight.

"What the hell," Aislin hisses from the floor as she gets her feet back underneath her. "Calm down Gemma, it's just me."

I lower my fist and turn on my lamp. "Oh my God, I'm so sorry." Suddenly realizing I'm wearing nothing but my underwear, I pick up the blanket and wrap it around me.

Aislin is wearing a plaid pajama set, her hair pulled up into a messy bun, and she has a jacket on. "Were you having a nightmare? You were making weird noises when I came in."

"Maybe… I honestly can't remember," I lie, sitting down on the bed with the blanket wrapped around me, thinking of the light vision and what it could mean. That Alex and I weren't going to survive?

"Gemma, you know you can talk to me about stuff," she says standing beside my bed. "I'm sure it's hard taking on all of this on your own."

"Thanks, but I'm not ready to talk about certain things just yet." I notice she has a bag draped over her shoulder. "Are you going somewhere?"

She nods, looking guilty. "And you are too... I mean, if you'll help me?"

"Help you with what?" I ask interestedly.

"With a spell."

"To remove the Mark of Malefiscus?"

"Hopefully," she says, taking her spell book out of the bag and opening it to a marked page. "I found a spell that could help... The Spell of Zaleena."

I squint down at the page. There's a drawing of a woman with her head angled back, her hands spanned to the side of her, her mouth open and a spirit rising out of it.

"And you think this spell's going to remove the Mark of Malefiscus?" I ask as she closes the book and tucks it back in her bag.

"The spell isn't exactly for removing a mark," she says. "But it's supposed to give the witch who performs the spell the gift of being able to separate and remove evil from those who are good."

"Is it dangerous?"

"I don't think so..." She seems uncertain. "It shouldn't be, but when it comes to magic, you never know." She shrugs. "You don't have to come if you don't want to. But I think your energy might come in handy because it's a really powerful spell. And I could use your company."

Weird. Was this how the start of friendships worked?

"Okay, let me get dressed and I'll go with you," I say. "But where exactly are we going?"

She hesitates then sighs. "To the cemetery."

***

The cemetery is located at the edge of town next to the forest and the hill line of the mountains. The moon and stars are covered by the clouds, the streets are lit up by lampposts, and the air is still, except for the scuffing of our shoes as we walk up the sidewalk.

"How intense is this spell going to be?" I ask, wrapping my jacket tightly around me. "You said you need power, so I'm guessing pretty intense."

"Yeah, it'll be pretty intense." She grows quiet, lost in her thoughts. I can tell something's bothering her and I'm about to ask her when she blurts out, "Gemma, do you like Laylen?" She sighs. "I don't mean to go all high school on you, but I just want—no—need to know if you like him as more than a

friend, like maybe the same way as you do with Alex."
She bites her lip, waiting for me to answer.

I feel extremely uncomfortable as I try to figure
out the right thing to say. "Laylen and I are just
friends," I finally tell her, wondering if that's the answer she wants.

"It's just that sometimes you two seem... I don't
know. You just seem happier when you're around
each other and then there was the whole biting
thing...."

"The biting thing we didn't want to happen... we
just got into a mess and then things got out of control." It feels like I need to say something that will
make her feel better but I can't figure out what that is.
"And I think we're more comfortable around each other because Laylen has always been honest with me
and he doesn't have painful history with me."

She looks hurt. "I get it... what I did to him in the
past is unforgivable."

"I wouldn't say that." I pause, drawing the hood of
my jacket over my head as the cool breeze picks up.
"Have you ever tried sitting down and talking to him?"

She shrugs, hugging her arms around herself.
"I'm worried what will happen... Of what he'll say."

"We'll you won't know until you try."

She glances at me. "Yeah, you're probably right, but can I ask you a question?"

"Um... sure."

"Have you forgiven Alex?"

"I..." I trail off, unsure how to respond because I honestly don't know if I have or not. "I'm not sure... maybe..."

"But you could see yourself doing so?" she asks, sidestepping a lamppost.

I nod and it feels right. "I think one day I could."

She pauses. "Gemma, I'm sorry for lying to you in the beginning, but I think if you'll give me another chance, you and I could be friends."

I start to smile, but then suddenly, something crashes behind us. We spin around, scanning the street, the yards, the trees, for where the noise came from, but there's nothing nearby.

"Keep your guard up," Aislin warns as we start walking again.

By the time we reach the cemetery, we've both grown edgy and that edginess only amplifies at the sight of the small area dotted with graves and sealed up by an iron gate. Trees shadow the grass and a gravel path runs through the entrance and up the center of it.

"Okay, this is really—"

Another thud from behind us, this time much louder and nearer. Aislin draws a knife out of her purse as we reel around again.

"What the hell?" Aislin lowers her knife. "What are you doing here?"

Aleesa stands beneath the light of the lamppost in pink pajamas, wide eyed and terrified. She opens her mouth and lets out a scream that echoes around us and causes dogs to bark in the distance.

"Stop!" Aislin conceals her hand over Aleesa's mouth. "Shhh… it's okay." After Aleesa settles down, Aislin moves her hand away. "What are you doing here?"

"I saw you leaving from out the window," Aleesa says. "And I followed you... I wanted to come with you."

Aislin frowns and snags hold of my arm, steering us away from Aleesa. "What should we do with her?" she whispers.

I shrug. "Take her with us, I guess. I mean, what else are we going to do? Take her back? The sun will be coming up in like an hour and I'm pretty sure we don't want to be sitting out in the cemetery performing a witch spell when it does."

"Yeah, I guess so, but still, she's so jumpy."

"Yeah, but considering her past that's under-standable."

Aislin appears guilt-ridden. "Yeah, you're right." She waves Aleesa over. "Come on, you can come with us."

Aleesa's eyes light up with happiness as she skips toward us and follows us into the cemetery. Aislin tells me we have to find a fresh grave, so we wander around the yard, looking for one and finally find one in the corner of the cemetery beneath a massive oak tree.

Aislin takes some black and red candles out of her bag and places them on the grass in a circle around the grave. "Alright, now we just need to sit in a circle around the candles," she says, lighting each candle with a lighter.

I take a seat in the cool grass and so do Aislin and Aleesa. Then Aislin sprinkles silver dust over the candles, making the color of the flames turn blood red.

She retrieves her spell book and opens it up. "Okay," she mutters, placing a red and green leaf in the center of our circle. "Are you guys ready for this?" she asks and must take our silence as a yes, because she takes a deep breath and chats. "*EGO dico ut ma-*

The Broken Visions

leena ut orior oriri ortus iterum. EGO dico ut maleena ut orior oriri ortus iterum!" Aislin screams, throwing her head back and elevating her hands above her head.

The candle's flames shift to yellow with a black center, casting an eerie glow around us, making every shadow seem like it's closing in on us. Then the flames grow bigger, more powerful, begin to ravel together until there's one giant flame stretching toward the sky. It takes the form of a woman, who rises above us and opens her hollow eyes.

"EGO dico ut maleena ut orior oriri ortus iterum!" Aislin yells again and the flame woman opens her mouth.

"Die!" she screeches with her mouth aimed at the sky and thunder booms even though there are no clouds in sight.

Aleesa screams as she jumps to her feet in a panic. Aislin's eyes snap wide as Aleesa sprints off through the cemetery toward the iron gate.

I look from the flaming woman to Aislin, hesitating. "Should I go get her?"

"Yes! Go!" Aislin cries, her hands out to the side, her eyes locked on the flame woman. "I'll be fine!"

Moments later, I'm on my feet and weaving around the graves as I chase down Aleesa. I lose track of her at one point but then spot her climbing over the fence and I speed up. As I reach the fence myself, I don't slow down, accelerating and springing up on my toes. With one quick leap, I'm up and over the fence, landing gracefully onto the gravel on the other side. Then I glance from left to right, searching for Aleesa, but she's nowhere. On a whim, I take off to my right, since it's the way to the house and I'm hoping she's headed back there. But as I'm barreling around the corner at full speed, I slam into a rock-hard surface. It almost knocks me to the ground, but I keep my balance and quickly regain my footing. But when I look up and see what I ran into, my heart stops.

A guy, tall, with skin like snow, and eyes as black as the night sky. He's dressed in black, hair as pale as the moonlight, and he smells like rust and salt. He sizes me up with his dark eyes and then smiles, flashing me his sharp, shiny fangs.

Chapter 21

"Well, what do we have here?" He grins as he stalks toward me. "I think I've ran into a bit of luck, haven't I?"

I start to back away, but he matches my movement, taking a step toward me every time I inch back, as if we're dancing. He pushes up the sleeves of his shirt and things get a little more frightening as I spot the Mark of Malefiscus branded on the back of his hand.

"Don't you know that wandering around at night is a dangerous thing? Especially at a place like this."

I need to do something quick to get myself out of this situation. Foresee my way back to the house? But what kind of person would I be to bail on Aislin like that?

Before I can come up with an answer, the vampire lunges for me. I instinctively lift my leg and kick him right between the legs. The vampire crumples to the ground, and taking advantage of his momentary weakness, I jump for the fence, but his fingers wrap around my ankle and he drags me back to the ground. I stumble forward and smack my head against the iron fence. I see stars all around me.

Focus, Gemma. Foresee your way to Aislin.

I shut my eyes and concentrate on the graveyard, but the vampire sinks his fangs into my leg and it feels like my skin is on fire. But I focus past the pain, grab a nearby stick off the ground, and flip over onto my back, plunging the stick into the vampire's back. He screams as I scream, my whole body feeling as though it's melting, my skin hot wax, my veins ash.

Blood. More stars. Alex. Then I'm sucked away into the darkness.

Chapter 22

When I open my eyes the sun is rising over the mountains and across the valley, painting the land with hues of pink and orange. Birds are chirping and a light breeze caresses my skin. I blink against the morning light, roll over to my stomach, and push myself to my feet. There's no sign of the vampire anywhere, but there's ash is scattered in the gravel just in front of my feet so I'm guessing when I stabbed him, it went through his heart.

I stretch my arms above my head and start walking, rounding the corner and crossing the cemetery, looking for Aislin, trying not to think about how I saw the mark on the vampire, which means Stephan's been getting more followers.

Aislin is in the spot where I left her, gathering her candles, looking pleased with herself. When she sees me, however, she frowns. "You didn't find her."

I give her a funny look. "Who...Oh! Aleesa. Shit." I glance back at the gate. "I completely forgot about her... I ended up running into some trouble."

"What kind of trouble?" Aislin asks as we hurry toward the entrance. "And why is your leg bleeding?"

I look down at my leg where blood is soaking through my jeans. Then I sigh and tell her what happened as we leave the cemetery and head back toward the house, searching yards and places nearby, looking for Aleesa.

"So he's marking vampires now?" Aislin shakes her head, frustrated. "God, this is getting out of control."

"I know," I say as we reach the corner of the street. "I need to get into that mapping ball and hopefully fix it."

We hop over the curb and start across the lawn toward a park, searching for Aleesa.

"I don't even want to think about where she'd go," Aislin says as she looks around the slide and swing area of the park

She's right. Aleesa is so new to the world and the idea that she's wandering around alone out here is frightening, especially if there are marked vampires and probably other things as well.

"What is that?" Aislin asks, squinting at the road.

I track her gaze to a Mazda parked beside the curb. "Shit."

The car door opens and Alex gets out, looking pissed. At first I think it's because we snuck out of the house without telling anyone, but then I see Aleesa sitting in the passenger side of the car.

"Did you two lose something?" he asks as he strides across the lawn toward us.

Aislin lets out a nervous laugh. "Yeah, where did you find her?"

Alex crosses his arms as he halts in front of us. "She came running into the house, screaming at the top of her lungs," he says. "When I got her to calm down, she told me you two were at the cemetery and that there was a crying fire woman there."

"Hmmm... that's weird," I say, trying to get us out of an Alex lecture. "Maybe she imagined it."

"It's okay, Gemma," Aislin says then looks confidently at her brother. "We were at the cemetery doing a spell which is going to hopefully remove the Mark of Malefiscus... I just need to try it out and see..." Aislin glances at me. "I'd like to try it out on your mom, but I understand if you want me to find another person to test it on first, just in case something happens. We could maybe track down that vampire."

"I think it's dead," I say. "At least I think that's what the ash was on the ground in front of me.

"Wait, what vampire?" Alex interrupts, with that look on his face that warns me he's about to go into

"Protect Gemma at All Cost Mode", so I quickly explain to him what happened and that I staked my very first vampire. And for the moment, he kind of looks proud of me, which is a first for me, from anyone. And it makes me feel kind of proud of myself, which is also a first.

Chapter 23

When we arrive at home, Aislin goes up to my mother's to try and see if she can get the mark off her. After Alex gives me a brief lecture on being more careful with myself then tells me that he thinks that I should start training, to get a better grasp on my fighting skills. But then says that he wants Laylen to do it, not giving an explanation why. But I know the answer—because he's trying to keep his distance from me.

So I agree and then go up to my room to change out of my pajamas and pull my hair out of my face. As I'm waiting for Laylen to show up, I decide to flip through the Foreseer book some more, to see if I can find the answer to the Purple Flame. It seems more important than ever now that I know the mark is traveling throughout the world.

But after searching through page after page, I grow frustrated and become desperate. I'm not sure if it's meant for what I'm about to do, but I decide it's worth the risk of trying.

"The Power of a Foreseer's Mind." I shut my eyes, focusing on seeing what I need to see, but am retaliated by light.

See past the light, see what you need to see. I'm not sure whose voice it is but I do as it says and look past the light.

The Purple Flame... the Purple Flame... the... Purple... Sharp pain erupts through my skull, like my head is cracking apart. I tip sideways on the bed and fall off of it. When I hit the floor, I slip deep inside my mind.

***

I'm energized, powerful, glowing. I can feel the energy inside me, about to combust and go out into the world. I'd be free from it and I realize I want to be free from it.

"Open your eyes, Gemma," a familiar voice whispers.

I open my eyes and then step back. I'm in the City of Crystal standing in front of the massive crystal ball that's about the size of a football stadium, flaring brightly within the enormous space of the cave. Attached to the crystal, solely by chains are people with tubes embedded in their skin, giving energy to the ball for the Foreseers.

"What you need is not in the book," the voice says to me. "It's in there. Touch it and you'll see."

I inch tentatively toward the crystal ball then taking a deep breath, I extend my hand toward it. My fingers are magnetized, begging us to connect. When I place my palm on it, the hot surface scorches my skin and a fire blazes through me. My heart slams against my chest as energy zips through my body, charging me. Powerful. I am powerful. I pull away and hold up my hand where a purple flame burns vibrantly in my palm.

"One of these days, you're going to have to figure things out without me," the voice says and this time I recognize who it belongs to.

I turn around and look behind me "Nicholas..."

I don't see him but I swear I detect the faint lingering scent of flowers and rain.

***

I bolt upright, lifting my hand in front of me. There's no fire burning from it, but I know what I have to do. I slip my shoes on and grab the Traveler's Ball that was left on my bed with the note. Maybe I should say something to someone. It'd probably be better if I did. But I know if I do then Alex will put up a fight so instead I shut my eyes, grasping onto the crystal ball filled with rubies and a few seconds later, I'm there.

Chapter 24

I land gracefully at the City of Crystal in the cave that has a charcoal ceiling that maroon crystals dangle from. Beneath the translucent floor, there's a midnight river flowing and carrying pieces of gold. And rubies wave across the snow-white walls.

I hurry and put the crystal ball into my pocket then sprint towards where the massive crystal ball is. My stomach churns as I enter the room and catch sight of the bodies strapped to the crystal illuminating with energy. Their eyes are shut, bodies still slack and lifeless. It makes me sick to see, but I don't look away. I hold my breath and block out everything but the flaming crystal ball they're attached to as I lean forward and place my hand to it, just like I did in the vision. Energy simmers through my veins and my heart accelerates so swiftly it aches inside my chest. It feels so different… like it's sucking the life from me instead of feeding me power.

I can't breathe…

It's killing me…

I jolt back and gasp as my eyes roll into the back of my head and my body begins to convulse. The crystal ball starts to hiss and sparks shoot out from it and land around my feet like embers. I start to think about how stupid I am for trusting a vision put in my head by Nicholas, but then I see my hand and the Purple Flame burning from it.

"Thank God," I say to myself as my body begins to calm down. I shut my hand as I distance myself from the crystal ball and the flame goes *poof*. When I open my hand again the flame ignites.

I'm in awe, opening and closing my hand a few more times before stopping in front of the door and taking the Traveler's Ball out of my pocket. I cast one last glance at the people trapped to the crystal ball and tell myself that one day I'll come back and free them, even if it means there will be no more Foreseers. The world can live without visions being read and will be better off too.

I smile at the thought and shut my eyes to leave this place. But right as I'm about to slip into the crystal ball, the door swings open and smacks me in the face. The crystal ball falls from my fingers and crashes against the floor, breaking the outer shell and rubies and water spills out onto the porcelain floor. Dyvinius enters the room wearing his silver robe that matches his eyes and a look that lets me know I'm in deep shit.

"Would you like to explain why you're here?" he asks, staring down at the broken crystal.

"A... um... would you believe me if I said I was lost?" I said innocently with a shrug.

He stares at me blankly. "No."

I deliberate my options. I could go all ninja on him, but kicking an old guy's ass doesn't seem right. So I let three seconds tick by, and then take off toward the massive crystal ball, hoping to wind around it and backtrack, then use my Foreseer power to get me out of here.

"Gemma." Dyvinius' calls out from right behind me. "I don't understand why you're running away from me."

Bull shit he doesn't.

I pick up my pace and smile when I see the door again. As I feel the power of the crystal ball fading, I decide there's enough room between us and close my eyes. But my own power is absent.

"There's no use trying," Dyvinius says in his monotone voice. "I have the place on lockdown. No one may leave or enter, even with a unique Foreseer gift like yours."

Dyvinius knows about my gift? This is not good.

I open my eyes, attempting to stay calm as I turn around and face him. "How do you know about my gift?"

He offers me a small smile as he stops in front of me. "You are your father's daughter. How could I not know?" He turns around, his silver robe swishing lightly across the floor. "This way please. We have much to talk about."

Having no choice but to follow, I trudge after him as he heads out the door and down a translucent crystal path that leads to his chamber. We go over a bridge paved with broken porcelain, underneath pillars, and through lofty silver doors where there's gemstone grass and the screen that shows visions. Right now there are images of people standing in the streets, which are on fire and filled with panic. It's startling to watch but Dyvinius seems unaffected by it.

When we reach the throne on the sapphire podium, he takes a seat and I stand in front of it. "Gemma, I'm not sure if you fully understand our laws," he says, overlapping his fingers and placing his hands onto his lap. "But we have certain rules to which Foreseers are supposed to abide to. The first and most important being never tamper with a vision. I'm not sure if you're aware of this or not, but your father broke this law a long time ago."

"If you knew who my father was," I say. "Then why didn't you say you did the first time you met me?"

"Because, back then you weren't who you are now," Dyvinius explains, resting back in his throne. "I see you heading down the same road as your father and I feel like it's important for you to understand."

"What road exactly?"

He contemplates something gravely. "Has anyone told you anything about your father?"

I shake my head. "Not really."

"Well he was a lot like you in the sense of having extraordinary power," Dyvinius says. "He could use the power of the Divination Crystal beyond the boundaries of an average Foreseer, beyond what even I can do, but he let it go to his head and did some unforgivable things. And because of that, he has to pay—he'll be a prisoner forever in the Room of Forbidden, alone in his own mind."

I shiver at the idea of my father being trapped in that place by himself for all eternity. "That seems a little harsh."

"Changing visions is a dangerous thing." Dyvinius says, his eyes matching the coldness in his tone. "And there has to be severe punishment for it... there has to be punishment whenever the rules are broken," he presses and I can see where this is going.

I skim the room looking for an escape route. I won't go down without a fight, even if it means beating up an old man.

"I hope you will take in what I said and obey the laws," he tells me. "I wouldn't want you to end up like you father."

"I won't end up like him," I assure him, but deep down I'm not sure what I'll end up like. Perhaps my father was once like me, said the same thing as me, but time changes people.

"Good." Dyvinius is pleased. "You may go." He motions toward the doors at the back of the room.

I don't question him. I hurry down the porcelain path for the silver doors, but stop when I see the image of Nicholas on the screen, standing beside me. We're just standing there looking at each other, my hand on my stomach and he has wicked grin on his face. And we're doing nothing as the streets burn around us.

"And Gemma," Dyvinius calls out, ripping my attention away from the screen.

I look back at him. "Yes."

"I look forward to the day when you come back for your training," he says in a way that makes me wonder if he thinks I'm not coming back.

I nod and glance back at the screen. The images have faded and now it's just blank. Shivering, I hurry out of the chamber and gladly leave the City of Crystal behind.

***

When I land back in house, I mishap and end up putting myself down in the living room where Alex is on the sofa, reading his mother's journal. My sudden appearance scares him so badly he jumps up and starts to reach for his knife. But once his brain processes that it's me he relaxes and lowers his hand.

"Fuck. You scared the hell out of me." He pauses, putting two and two together. "What...Where have you... When did you leave the house?"

Not sure what to say, I give him an innocent look, raise my arm, and open my hand. The Purple Flame ignites, bright and fierce, channeling power through me.

His anger shifts into amazement as he sets the journal down. "Where... how did you..."

I close my hand and the flame simmers out. Then I sit down on the sofa and tell him everything that happened, minus a few details.

"So this is it then?" Alex sinks down on the sofa beside me. "You're just going to go into the mapping ball and if it all works out, the vision will be changed and the world's future will go back to normal?"

"Yeah, that's the best case scenario," I say, frowning. "Although, I'm starting to doubt more and more that my father was telling me the truth... the way Dyvinius was talking about him... he made him seem so evil." My jaw tightens and I'm not sure whether I feel sad or angry. "Just how my mom said he was."

"Hey," Alex says, hooking a finger under my chin and turning my head toward him. "Just because Dyvinius doesn't like your dad, doesn't mean he's bad. We need to find stuff out for ourselves before we decide that."

"I know." I release a shaky breath. "It's just hard to hear how people talk about him... and Dyvinius... he was speculating that I'd turn out like him."

"That will never happen." He is being so kind, so caring. "Just because your father's evil, doesn't mean you'll turn out evil."

"Yeah, you're right," I say. "I mean, look at you. You have the worst father in the world but you turned out alright."

He looks uncertain of how to respond, his eyes greener than they've ever been, his breathing quickening. "You don't know half the things I've done," he whispers. "I might just be as bad as him."

I shake my head. "No, you're not." I take a deep breath, deciding to move past this heavy stuff, the prickle guiding me to my decision. "How about we make a promise to move past this?" I stick out my hand to shake on it. "That we'll let go of the past and focus on the future, which is what life's about anyway, right?"

He stares down at my hand and then his gaze interlocks with mine. "Alright, I promise." But he doesn't take my hand. Instead he leans forward and presses his lips to mine, so delicately, so tenderly that it warms my soul.

"Can I show you something," he whispers, his mouth hovering above mine. "Before we go save the world. I promise it's not too far away and it won't take very long."

I nod without a second thought, realizing I'd go anywhere with him. Deep down I can feel that my emotions for him are headed into a dangerous territory. And I should walk away, but whatever I'm feeling for him owns me and my actions so I get up and take his hand.

"Okay, lead the way."

"Actually, you have to," he says, giving my hand a squeeze. "I need you to take me to the vision of when I first saw you in the parking lot at your college—when we were technically reunited again."

Reluctantly I do so, not because I'm afraid of what I might see, but afraid of what I won't see, in myself.

"Just trust me," he says as if he can read my mind.

And so I do, taking us away.

Chapter 25

It's hard for me to pinpoint the exact time, simply because I was unemotional for part of the vision and that time in my life is hard to remember. It always felt like nothing was happening, because nothing was. I had a broken soul, no connection to humanity; I was just a ghost roaming the world.

But I manage to get us to that time and place, dropping us safely into the middle of the campus yard where I had been observing people. The sunlight is trickling through the trees, the air is cool, and in the middle of it all is a sad looking violet eyed girl, sitting on a bench, looking lost, out of it, almost like a zombie.

"My eyes look so empty," I note, crossing the yard to get a closer look. Alex is still holding my hand and follows me, gripping onto me tightly.

"They do," he agrees. "But in just a few minutes you won't."

I wait, watching the vision form of myself sit there staring at people until finally she gives up and gets up to leave. She strolls across the campus yard, with no real direction or purpose, her bag over her shoulder, as she gazes into nothingness. And then she reaches the parking lot, drops her keys, picks them up, and start glancing around with a perplexed look on her face.

The moment that changed my life forever.

"I remember this part," I whisper. "It felt like someone was watching me."

"I was," Alex says then points over to his cherry red 1969 Camaro parked toward the back beneath the trees. The vision form of himself is standing by the front of the car with his hands tucked into his pockets, looking nonchalant at first glance, but upon further assessment...

"You look nervous," I say.

"I was," he replies, his eyes not on himself, but on me—the real me. "Because I was about to do something really wrong."

"You mean get close to me?" I ask as his thumb gently grazes the inside of my wrist.

He shakes his head once, eyes forward, jaw set tight. "I mean, let your soul heal and let you be emotional again."

"But you didn't know it was going to happen." I watch as the vision form of me touches the back of her neck. It's about to happen. My emotions are going to rush back to me and I'm going to start crying for the first time in my life.

"Yeah, I did." He utters it so quietly his voice nearly gets carried away in the wind. He lifts his hand and points it at the vision form of himself, which is still in front of the car, but now his lips are moving.

"What are you saying?" I ask as I watch the vision form of myself feel the rush of emotion and tears pour out of her eyes. I want to cry with her, bawl my eyes out because I can still remember the emotional pain that I didn't understand at the time.

"Stuff I can't share with you yet, because it might break you again," he says, glancing at me from the corner of my eye and I swear to God it feels like my stomach lurches up my throat. "I was told by a Foreseer I could help you return to... well, you. The emotional you that you should have been all along."

"But you were so against me feeling things all the time. It doesn't make any sense."

"It's because I was conflicted." He faces me, taking both of my hands in his. "I kept having these dreams of you drowning and I was just watching you, not helping. It kept happening for years and finally I couldn't take it anymore, so I went and sought help." He glances over at the vision form of himself again.

"Afterward, I felt like I'd done something wrong, but at the same time right… I was really confused."

I stare at him for a moment and can tell he's avoiding eye contact with me, not because he's lying but because he's putting himself out there and is vulnerable. I look over at the vision form of him, watching the vision form of me on the ground, crying, drowning in emotions.

"I wanted to go to you," he whispers. "I debated it over and over again in my head, but the bad side of me won."

"I don't think there was a bad side of you in this moment," I tell him. "Or now."

He doesn't say anything, letting go of my hands, and raking his fingers through his hair. "Well, I'm glad you think so." The vision form of him drives off and the vision me gets to her feet, before he speaks again. "We should go back," he says quietly. "I just wanted you to know the truth."

"Thank you," I tell him, choking back an emotion fighting to be revealed. "Not just for telling me the truth, but for giving me back my soul and emotions."

The corners of his lips tug upward, but it's barely a smile. "Don't thank me. They never should have been stolen to begin with."

Chapter 26

I try not to think about what Alex showed me, but it's difficult. All this time, he'd been the one that freed me. It was amazing and yet at the same time, heart-breaking. After we leave the vision, we go back to the house, landing in the living room quietly. I refuse to let go of his hand, even when he walks over to the sofa and flops down. He doesn't seem to mind though, sketching his fingers lightly across my knuckles as he stares out fingers entangled together.

"I want you to be careful when you do this," he says. "When you go into the mapping ball. And prepare yourself for the worst case scenario."

"I will," I promise him. "And I promise I won't alter any visions unless I think it's the right thing to do." I pause. "I'm hoping, though, if I do, it'll realign everything else and maybe things won't be so out of whack."

He looks up at me. "You mean with the section of time your father reset?" he asks and I nod. He contemplates something. "Maybe you should put that one back too, just so everything is back to the way it was."

I shake my head swiftly, my hand tightening on his. "No way."

"Gemma, I—"

"I won't do it," I cut him off, maintaining his gaze. "I won't do anything where you die. And besides, if I change my father's vision that stuff might never happen anyway."

We both grow silent, realizing that if I change it, what we have right now might be lost.

"Be careful," he says in a hoarse whisper, cupping the back of my head. "Please, just don't do anything that'll hurt yourself."

I nod and then he kisses me, in a way he's never kissed me before. Slow and sensual, with meaning behind it, flooding me with tingles and butterflies and causing my pulse to throb under my flesh. It's like he's saying good-bye to whatever we have now, in case it disappears. I wish the kiss could go on forever, life would be so easy if it could, but it ends, way too soon in my opinion.

"Should we wake everyone up?" I ask Alex as I lean forward and collect the mapping ball from the coffee table.

"That's up to you," he says, drawing a line up and down the back of my neck.

It sounds like a simple question, yet it's not. To say good-bye is painful and will probably upset everyone, but what I might end up doing in the mapping ball could potentially erase everything we have and I might not even know who they are in the end.

"I'm going to be an optimist for once." I cup the crystal ball in my hand and it illuminates vibrantly. "And not say good-bye so I can tell myself that this is all going to work out…. This will all be fine."

It has to be. I have a mom upstairs, branded by the mark of evil, a beautiful vampire friend, who is so sad my heart breaks for him, a witch friend who is afraid to show who she really is, and a gorgeous guy I feel so much for yet if those emotions get too strong, we could die. But hopefully, I have the power to remove the pain and give them a future without death, loneliness, and despair.

So squaring my shoulders, I walk to the middle of the living room. I open my hand and let the Purple Flame erupt from my palm. Alex's eyes light up with worry and I can sense a panicked protest coming.

"Don't worry." I give him a small smile. "This is what I was made to do."

And with those last words, I place the mapping ball in my hand into the Purple Flame. It flashes, shaking the walls and the floor as the light ripples around the room. My whole body flares up into flames and then I'm being tugged inside the ball.

Chapter 27

When I open my eyes, I'm still in the living room, the Purple Flame burning from my hand as the mapping ball sparkles in it, hissing and crackling as if it's a hollow log.

"It didn't work." Alex frowns disappointed, yet relieved.

I frown, too. "But I felt it work."

Alex leans closer to inspect the mapping ball without touching it. "Maybe the Purple Flame wasn't what we needed. You did get the idea from a random note left on your bed. And we don't even know who left the note."

Someone who smells an awful lot like Nicholas, I want to say, but don't want to look insane. "Yeah, but, the Purple Flame existed like the note said." I glance at the flame in my hand, dancing and swaying, fueling my body with power I can't figure out how to use. "It's got to be used for it."

We stare at the flame, trying to put the missing pieces together. Finally, I sigh, remove the mapping ball from my hand, and smother the Purple Flame out. "Dammit, I thought I had it."

"Maybe that's the problem," Alex states as I put the mapping ball down on the coffee table, frustrated. "Maybe you're trying too hard. Sometimes your power doesn't work when you drain yourself." He delicately grazes his finger across my jawline and I shiver. "Maybe you should go lie down and try to sleep for a bit, and then try again when you wake up."

I want to protest because sleeping feels like the last thing I need to do, but I nod, deciding I'm going to try something else, something I'm not ready to share with him. "Okay, give me like a few hours."

He turns to me as I'm walking out, his lips quirking with amusement, something I haven't seen in a few days. "You want some company?"

I shake my head and make myself disregard the hurt that flashes across his face at my rejection. "Sorry, but I won't sleep if you're in there." I force a smile and he relaxes slightly.

I dash up the stairs and into my room, locking the door behind me, not believing what I'm about to do because it makes it seem like I might be losing my mind.

"Nicholas," I whisper as I trail around my room, glancing in all the nooks and corners. "Are you in here?" I anticipate a response, but all I can hear is the wind howling outside. "If you can hear me, please say something… I have questions about the note I think you left on my bed."

Nothing. I surrender from talking to the dead, flopping down onto the bed on my back and staring up at the ceiling, just like I used to do when I was emotionally numb, only this time my mind is racing. "I must really be getting desperate," I mutter.

"The answers to your problems aren't in your ceiling," a low pitch voice suddenly says.

My eyes widen as I hastily sit up, skimming my room for whoever spoke to me, but I don't see anyone. "Who's there… Nicholas, is that you?" It doesn't sound like him, but I'm not discounting the idea just yet.

"That's not the question you should be asking." The voice *tsks*. "You're not focusing on the problem."

I lower my feet to the floor, looking everywhere when I speak because I'm not sure where to focus— the voice seems like it's encompassing me. "Are you the one who left the note?"

They make this buzzer sound. "Wrong question again."

I climb off my bed, on guard. "Why does it sound like you're disguising your voice like a game show host?"

"Gemma." They sound so disheartened. "You need to stop focusing on other things and start focusing on saving the world."

"That's kind of what I've been doing." I move over to my closet and throw it open, but it's vacant.

"Come on, Gemma, ask me the right question."

"Okay." I shut the closet door, turn around, and lean against it. "How can I get into the mapping ball?"

"*Ding. Ding.* We have a winner." A pause. "With the Purple Flame."

"I already have the Purple Flame." I draw back the curtain and peer out the window. It's raining outside, puddles and mud covering the grass, sidewalks, and streets. "It didn't work."

Silence.

I sigh, turning away from the window and checking under my bed. "Okay, how do I get the Purple Flame to work with the mapping ball?"

"*Ding, ding,* there you go," they say with exaggerated cheerfulness. "Now look at your arm."

I kneel up and elevate my arm in front of me. "Okay... it looks like an arm, except for the ugly olive-green lines tracing my skin..." I flip my hand over and look at the hideous lines Stasha's death left on my flesh. "Wait, is that what's causing it not to work?"

"You can't restore life with death in your hand," they tell me in a serious tone.

"Strangely enough, that actually makes sense. But the death in my skin is permanent, so how can I make it go away?"

"Go back and ask her to take it away." The voice is fading.

"Are you crazy?" I ask. "Stasha will kill me."

No response. No annoying *ding, dings*.

I sigh begrudgingly. I guess I'm going to Stasha's.

***

Paying a visit to a girl who tried to murder me makes me a little bit edgy so I decide I need backup. The best person for the job is Laylen because a) unlike Alex, he's never dated Stasha, therefore his presence will keep jealous fits to a bare minimum, and b) Laylen is immortal so Stasha's touch can't kill him.

It's still early as I tiptoe down the hallway to the room Laylen sleeps in. Alex is downstairs talking to Aislin about Aleesa, they're newfound sister, and I decide to let them be for now, let them have their moment where they're not worrying about the end of the world.

I crack open the door and peek my head into Laylen's room. "Laylen," I whisper as I turn the light on and rap my hand on the doorway. "I need your help."

He jumps out of the bed, arms flailing, ready to attack, but calms down when he sees it's me. "Fuck, Gemma. What the hell are you doing?" He exhales, unstiffening. "You really have an act for sneaking up on me when I'm asleep, don't you?"

As the blanket falls from his body, my eyes travel across his lean chest and carved muscles, the side decorated with a black ink tattoo of symbols running vertical. "I'm sorry," I say, blinking my gaze off his body. "I should have knocked first."

"It's okay," he says as he gets out of his bed, wearing only his boxers. I'll admit he's sexy as hell. Long legs, tattoos hidden in places I'd never thought of—I want to touch them all, but the thing that stops me is Alex and how I feel for him, which is mind-blowingly terrifying. "Did you need something?" He grabs a pair of jeans off the floor and puts them on.

"Yeah, I need your help with… something."

He buckles the studded belt around his pants. "With what?"

"I need you to come with me to Stasha's," I say, watching him tug a black shirt over his head.

258

"I don't think that's such a good idea." He looks down at the olive-green lines scarring my arm as he ruffles his hair into place. "Considering what happened the last time you went there."

"But I need to. The Purple Flame won't work unless I do."

"Wait, you got the Purple Flame? When?"

"Oh, I guess I need to back up a few steps, don't I?"

He nods and we sit down on the bed. I start from the beginning, telling him what's happened while he's been napping.

"So you think the scars on your arms are what's stopping the Purple Flame from working?" he asks after I finish explaining. I exclude the details of how I received the information about the scars. Laylen is understanding, but telling him that a talk-show-host voice told me about it and that I'm pretty sure it was Nicholas disguising his voice is something I don't want to share with anyone *ever*.

I nod. "Yeah, I'm pretty sure."

He sweeps his blue-tipped bangs away from his forehead. "How do you know that's what's wrong? I mean, it could be a thousand different things." He eyes me over with skepticism. "Why do I get the feeling you're keeping something from me? Something about how you got the information?"

"Would you believe me if I said that a little birdie told me?"

"Gemma," he starts, but I stop him.

"Look, I get that you want to know, but I just need you to trust me." I carry his gaze. "It's for the best that you don't know."

I feel a splash of emotion current through me and for the briefest second I feel like tearing off Laylen's clothes and touching him all over. But I'm not sure if it's stemming from myself or if Laylen is feeling something at the moment and his emotion manipulation gift is accidentally seeping into me, and it makes me feel slightly uncomfortable, if he feels something for me as more than a friend. Could that be possible?

"Okay, if that's what you think needs to be done, then let's go to Stasha's." He rubs his jawline with a thoughtful expression "But if she tries to kill you again, I might have to resort to violence."

"And that's perfectly okay with me." I grab his hand, tugging him up as I stand. He towers above me as I shut my eyes and moments later we are being swept away.

Chapter 28

We land in Stasha's living room between the two floral sofas and the brick fireplace, surrounded by the creepy vines growing along the walls and the ceiling.

"Careful." I point up at the vines dangling above us. "They come alive. They attacked me the last time I was here."

Laylen pulls a disgusted face. "Leave it to Alex to date such a weirdo."

"Hey," I say, offended, but then realized Alex and I have never officially dated.

Laylen waits for me to say something, but when I don't, he lets go of my hand and we wander around the house. We check every room and the kitchen, but Stasha is nowhere.

"I don't think she's here," I say as we return to the living room.

"Good observation," he jokes and I stick out my tongue amazed at how the tension has crumbled between us. I'm beginning to see that kind of up and down pattern between Laylen and me and wonder what it could lead to in the future, good or bad. "But that just means we can take her by surprise."

"I like the way you think."

He flops down on the sofa and gets comfortable as he stretches his arms out on the back. "So did you know Aislin came to me and said she was sorry for everything?"

"That's a little weird." I'm not surprised, after the talk we had on our way to the cemetery. "But good, right?"

He wavers, gaze fixed on me as I stroll around the living room looking at photos, some of which are of Alex and Stasha and they make me feel ill to my stomach because they actually look happy together. "Yeah, but I was wondering where it all of a sudden came from?" He pauses. "Did you have anything to do with it?"

I shrug, keeping my back at to him as I stare at one picture in particular of Stasha kissing Alex on the cheek. He's rolling his eyes but he looks content and it kind of gets under my skin a little. "Does it really—"

"Shhh…" Laylen hisses, leaping up from the sofa. "I think I hear something."

We freeze, listening to the sound of footsteps heading toward the front door. Then we run down the hallway, making it just in time as the front door swings open. I crouch behind Laylen who hunkers down at the edge of the wall.

"I don't know why he made me take one of you stupid things." Stasha slams the door and I hear her keys land on the table. "I mean, it's not like you do any good. And I can't even hear what you're saying. And don't ruin my plants," she snaps at someone, clearly not alone. "I need them to keep me alive." There's a pause and then she says, "This is ridiculous. Do you leak ice or something?"

Laylen's head whips in my direction. *Ice*, he mouths as the temperature drops and frost begins to glaze the floor around us. I'd be afraid, but after taking so many of them down at the castle, it doesn't seem as terrifying.

"Do you want to take down Stasha or the Death Walker?" I whisper in Laylen's ear as the ice slips under our feet and along the wall behind us.

"I'll take death girl, since you've proven you can handle a Death Walker," he whispers back. "Besides, her touch won't kill me."

I nod and then take out a knife from my pocket. Then Laylen peeks around the corner and looks back at me. "Okay… the Death Walker's on the couch. And Stasha's watering her plants."

I poise the knife in front of me and Laylen lifts his hand, counting down on his fingers... *three... two... one...*

We jump out from the hallway and take them by surprise. The Death Walker's eyes flash yellow as it towers to its feet. Stasha drops her pail she has in her hand and water spills on the floor. "What the hell?" she says, her face reddening with anger.

The Death Walker instantly marches toward me as I step forward with the knife out in front of me while Laylen goes for Stasha. The Death Walker's eyes flash murderously as pieces of its rotting flesh fall from its face. As it approaches me, it throws back its head and lets out a shriek before charging. Like at the castle I feel in control and powerful as I dodge out of its way. But it turns around and circles back. So I stop moving and its eyes flicker as I lunge for it. Its hands shoot out toward my neck, but I duck and evade it, skidding on my knees across the floor. Then it backs up, trying to get out of my reach. I get to my feet and swing the knife at it, but miss and cut its cloak.

I don't give up, swinging back around and as it lets out another wail, I stab the knife into its chest and drop low to the ground as its breath puffs through the air while its body sways to the side. Then its eyes burn out and it tips over, hitting the floor with a thunderous boom. But I know it's not dead, just passed out, because it's Immortal and I don't have the Sword of Immortality.

I whirl around, relieved to see that Laylen has Stasha pinned up against the wall. He holds her there by her shoulders and she glares at him.

"You're messing up my hair," she whines when Laylen shoves her against the wall harder.

I hop over the unconscious Death Walker and go over to them, Stasha's eyes immediately narrowing on me. "Well look who was stupid enough to come back," she says "What? Did you not get enough of me the first time?"

I point the tip of my knife at her throat. "You know, it really doesn't seem like you're in much of a position to be such a bitch."

Stasha gives me a dirty look. "This is such bull shit. You have nothing over me."

I move the knife closer until it clips her skin and draws blood.

She winces, pressing herself closer the wall. "Fine, what do you want?"

I raise my scarred arm. "I want you to take your death out of my arm."

She shakes her head. "No way. You deserve it there—you deserve more pain than even I can inflict."

The sight of Laylen's fangs descending from his blood red lips causes her eyes to nearly pop out of head. "I think you're the one who might deserve something a little more painful." He pauses. "Now I know what you're thinking. Vampire bites don't hurt, in fact they feel good. But since I can manipulate your emotions, I can make it painful for you." He grins at her, flashing his pointed fangs.

Stasha is pissed, but I can tell he's scaring her. She leans away, turning her head to the side. "Fine. I'll remove my death from your hand," she snaps. "But you two are lucky that that stupid monster's ice froze over my plants, otherwise this would have gone down differently."

"And if you try to kill her instead of removing the death, I'll drain you of all your blood, got it?" Laylen says with his fangs still out.

"Got it," Stasha replies through gritted teeth.

Laylen slightly loosens his grip so Stasha can slip off her one of her gloves. "Give me your arm," she says to me.

Hesitantly, I extend my arm to her and she enfolds her fingers around my wrist. Within seconds, the olive-green lines fade away, until my skin is back to its normal color. I let out a breath of relief as she with-draws her hand, but then gasp as I catch sight of something on her wrist.

A black triangle around a red symbol.

Laylen tracks my gaze and he shoves Stasha back against the wall roughly. "Where did you get that?" he demands.

Stasha looks down at the mark on her wrist. "This? I've always had it you dumbass."

Laylen shakes his head. "That's not possible... I've know you for long enough to know it hasn't al-ways been there."

"Yes, it has," she says in a condescending tone. "I've had it since the day I was born, but apparently you're too stupid to remember."

"Alex would have seen it when he was dating you," I say, gripping the knife in my hand, fighting the compulsion to stab her. "And he would have men-tioned it by now."

Stasha laughs sharply. "Yeah right. He's lied to me more than anyone in my life and I'm sure he's do-ing it to you."

Laylen starts to say something, but then the Death Walker starts to stir, waking up.

"We need to go," I say and reach for Laylen's hand.

"What about her?" he asks. "What should we do to her?"

I shrug. "Whatever you want?"

Laylen considers this but not for very long and he knocks her out by clocking her in the head with his own. Stasha falls to the floor, her eyes rolling into the back of her head as the Death Walker charges at us. But I'm already blinking us away.

Chapter 29

When we get back to the house, Laylen and I decide that the best thing to do is go downstairs and simply ask Alex if he knew about the mark. We could sit there and try to figure it out ourselves but at this point I am tired of dithering around things.

In the living room, Aislin has herbs and candles in front of her as she reads a page on her spell book. She hasn't had any luck yet getting the mark off my mother and has been burying herself in trying to solve what went wrong. It shows through her red eyes, bags under them, and, she's in her pajamas, her hair a mess. Alex is sitting beside Aleesa as she watches something on television, but it's clear he's not paying attention, gazing off into empty space.

When he looks up at me, he sort of flinches as if seeing me is painful for him. I simply raise my arm up and show that the lines are gone, figuring that's the best way to start this conversation.

He drops the remote onto the table, stunned. "How did you get them off?"

I glance at Laylen beside me and he gives me an encouraging look. "We paid Stasha a little visit," I tell him.

"What?" He's baffled and so is Aislin, who looks up at us, confounded. "When?"

"Just barely," I explain. "I had a little hunch that if they were gone, the Purple Flame might work."

"I wish you would have said something before you took off," he says, trying to keep his need to be dominant and controlling intact.

"Yeah, I know, but you were talking to Aislin and I didn't want to bother you." I glance from Laylen to Aislin, who are listening intently, then back to Alex. "Can I talk to you alone for a minute?"

He gives me a funny look, but goes into the kitchen with me without asking questions.

"Okay, what's going on?" He reclines against counter, arms folded. "You're acting weird."

"When Laylen and I—" I start, but a strange noise escapes his throat, like he's choking back a cough. "What was that noise you just made?" I inch toward him, attempting to pick up on his vibe.

"You really want to know?" he asks and I nod. In three long strides, he's stolen the space between us and backed me up into the counter. An arm comes down on each side of me, trapping me between him. "My problem is that every time you have a problem, you run off with Laylen. And it's driving me crazy. After how far we've come... after the things I've shared with you... I thought by now you'd come to me when you needed help—it's what I'm good at."

"I'm sorry, but it seemed better to take Laylen since he can't die from Stasha's touch." I suck in a loud breath. "And she's your ex-girlfriend."

"I already told you she never meant anything to me."

"Yeah, but you clearly meant something to her—she has pictures of you two all over her house."

He presses his lips together. "What do you want me to do?" He pauses and I can tell the way his eyes crinkle that he's trying not to smile. "Go to her house and steal all the photos away, because I will. Just say the word."

I shake my head, attempting to stay annoyed. "No, that'd be silly." I pause and his smile starts to break through, so I reach forward and playfully pinch him on the side. "This isn't funny."

Now he's grinning as he touches the spot where I pinched him. "It kind of is." He brushes a strand of hair out of my face. "You're cute when you're jealous."

"That's not what this is about," I tell him then re-member what I'm really supposed to be discussing with him. "Did you know Stasha has the Mark of Ma-lefiscus?"

The shock on his face is too real and I know right away that he didn't. "No, she doesn't... I'd know...."

"She does, though. I saw the mark on her wrist, and she told us she's had it since she was born."

"That's not possible." He shakes his head, grip-ping onto the counter. "I'd know if she did."

I hated that he would know. "So I'm guessing that either he recently put it on her and tampered with her mind to make her think she's had it forever, or this is another case of the butterfly effect from resetting time..." I look down at my hand and flex my fingers. "It's time for me to go see what I can do about this." I open my hand and the flame smolders.

"You think it's going to work now?" Alex asks, the flame reflecting in his bright green eyes.

"There's only one way to find out." I march out of the kitchen without putting the fire out and Laylen, Aislin, and Aleesa all jump back. I scoop up the map-ping ball and place it in my hand as they all watch. It fits perfectly and my skin begins to sizzle. Energy tor-rents through me, violet, passionate, untamed. My eyes snap wide as searing heat spills through my veins, gives me an indescribable power, and then sucks me into the glass.

Chapter 30

It's so dark it makes the air thick and heavy, bearing down on me and crushing my body. I have to be dead. There's no way I could be alive with this much pain. But then I open my eyes and see the most beautiful sight I've ever seen before me, like I landed outside of the world, where the stars shine. They are everywhere. Above me. Below me. As far as my eyes can see.

"It's so gorgeous," I whisper in wonderment. But as I start to wander across the stars, my heart sinks in despair. There is no sign of memories or anything that will lead me to them.

But as if answering me, one of the stars just in front of my feet illuminates. I hop back as light flows out of it and casts against the darkness like a movie screen. At first it's blank, but then people appear on it. A man probably about twenty years old with dark brown hair and violet eyes—my dad. He's talking to an older woman with flowing auburn hair, wearing a pressed tan dress—Sophia.

"Well, I don't see how that would be possible," Sophia tells my father as they hike up the grassy hill toward the grey stone castle at the top. "Jocelyn's too busy with things. And she's supposed to be taking her Keeper's test soon."

"I understand your concern," my dad replies, attempting to dazzle her with a charming smile. "But I promise you, I won't keep her out too long."

Sophia fixes him with a stern gaze, one that I had seen many times, not at all affected by my dad's charm. "Well, I'll have to think about it and discuss it with her father, but we'll see."

My father stops on the hill, beaming. "That's all I'm asking for."

Sophia gives him a curt nod and then hurries to the front door of the castle, leaving him on the hill. My father turns, picks up a rock, and chucks it into the lake, making the water ripple. He looks happy, not like someone who is about to cause the end of the world.

"He couldn't have always been evil,' I say. "There's just no way."

The scene swirls back into the star. Not the vision I'm looking for, but it was interesting to see my dad, just a normal guy, wanting to ask my mom out.

Suddenly, another star lights up against the darkness just a few feet away. On the screen, my father is the main focus, about the same age as he was in the last one. He's sitting next to my mom who looks around the same age as him. Her makeup is done and her hair is curled up and they're in the corner, huddled together, with a stack of books by their feet.

"I still don't understand why you have to help him," my mother says to my father. "It doesn't make any sense.

My father takes her hands in his. "Everything will be okay, Jocelyn. Stephan assures me that once I help him, we can be together; that he'll make it so your parents won't have any problems with us wanting to get married."

My mother swallows hard. "Julian, please don't do this... I'm begging you"

"It'll be alright." My dad cups her face in his hands and leans closer. "Stephan just needs my help with something and then this will all be over. And you and I can begin our happy life together."

She looks like she wants to say something but can't. "Your help you with what? Has he even told you?"

"He hasn't, but I'm sure it'll be fine."

My mother itches at her wrist, right where the Mark of Malefiscus is now, but her long-sleeved shirt covers it up. She keeps scratching and scratching like she's trying to claw her skin off.

"Please don't go, Julian," she pleads. "I'm begging you not to."

"I have to otherwise, I'll never have this." And then he kisses her.

I let out a shaky breath as the picture fades back into the star. They seemed so normal and in love, not evil or marked, not about to end the world.

I move to the next star and wait for it to light up, wondering what I'm going to see next. When the screen shines across the blackness, my body tenses. Stephan is sitting at a long mahogany table, dressed in black, his hair slicked to the side, and he's grinning. Across from him, is my dad with his arms on the table, the sleeves of his blue shirt rolled up revealing that his arms are mark free.

"I have to say, Julian, I'm surprised you showed up." Stephan says. "Jocelyn must mean a lot to you."

My dad shifts in the chair and then tucks his arms underneath the table, anxious. "Is it true you can create marks? Can you really mark me as a Keeper?"

I nearly fall to the ground. That's what he wanted? He wanted Stephan to make him a Keeper?

"Hmmm..." Stephan grazes his finger across the scar on his cheekbone, musing. "Is it true there's a way for a Foreseer to change a vision?"

My dad's expression plummets. "I—I don't think so."

Stephan slants forward in his chair toward my father. "You know what I hate more than anything, Julian?" he asks in an icy tone, his eyes darkening. "People who lie. I can't stand fucking liars."

"I'm not lying, sir," my dad says, his voice faltering. "I swear, I'm not."

Stephan digs his fingernails into the wood of the table, as if channeling his anger there. "I understand there are rules that the Foreseers have that forbid you to tell me." He scoots back and then rounds the table, halting in front of my father. "Give me your arm, Julian."

"What?" My dad gapes up at Stephan. "Why?"

"Give. Me. Your. Arm," Stephan repeats in a firm tone.

My dad exhales loudly then extends out his arm. Stephan retrieves a knife from the table and without warning, plunges it into my father's forearm. "*Vos es venalicium!*"

My dad whimpers out in pain, his fingers moving for the knife. But it's too late. A mark appears on his wrist as blood seeps out of his skin and dribbles onto the floor. "Why did you... I don't understand," my father stammers, pressing his hand to the wound.

Stephan tosses the knife onto the table, grinning. "Now you have no choice but to help me."

My father removes his hand from his arm and gasps in horror. Along his forearm, there's a black triangle outlining a red symbol.

"But you said you would give me the Keeper's mark." My father turns his arm toward Stephan. "What the hell is this?"

"Oh, you'll soon find out," Stephan says darkly.

The light diminishes into the star as my knees give out and I sink onto the starry ground. My mother lied. My father didn't want power. He wanted to be with her. He thought he was becoming a Keeper. Why did my mom lie about this? Or didn't she know the truth? Was the only story she knew from Stephan's point of view?

But then Stephan had told me that a person had to possess evil blood for the mark to work, so either my father has some sort of evil hidden in him, or Stephan was lying about that and he can put the mark on anyone. Both scenarios make me shiver.

The man has ruined too many lives and it's time to stop him. Filled with determination, I push to my feet. I need a way to find out a way to figure out which star held the right memory. I sort through my memories, trying to think of something that may have been mentioned in the past. Nicholas and my dad both said something about my mind having the answers. If I could just *see* which one holds the right memory... I get an idea as I think of the Foreseer book and concentrate on not seeing the stars, but seeing *the one* that carries the memory of my dad when he altered the vision that will lead to the destruction of earth. The stars begin to glimmer, playing a melody of color, and then a silver cloud rises from the ground. I move back as it slithers across the stars like a snake and into the darkness and I chase after it, weaving around stars, until it finally comes to a stop above a lavender one that shines brighter than all the others. The magical cloud swoops into the air and then swan-dives down into the star. I stop and wait for the screen to light up, but no light or movie clip appears so I lean over and peer into it. There's a faint light emitting from the center and hesitantly, I bend down and brush my fingers against it. Energy jolts through my body and the ground trembles. The ground below my feet cracks and then begins to break. I let out a scream as the entire starry area around me crumbles, taking me with it.

Chapter 31

When I land, it's soft and I'm breathless. I'm on a hill with my back to the Keeper's castle, and in front of me are the lake and the trees, crisp with ice and frost, the water frozen, the sky cloudy and grey. And Death Walkers are everywhere.

My dad comes walking down the hill toward the lake. He's still around twenty but he's wearing the same silver robe he was wearing in the Room of Forbidden. His face is solemn, his violet eyes fixed on the lake with worry shadowing them. He doesn't seem to notice me as he passes by, so I follow after him, figuring I'm in vision form.

"Where is it?" he mutters as he halts at the icy shore of the lake.

Death Walkers creep out from the trees, their black cloaks dragging across the snow, their yellow eyes reflecting against the ice. I shiver as the ground quivers with the beat of their march and when Stephan emerges from the forest, not too far off from where we stand. He has on a black cloak with the hood over his head and his eyes seem to light up in delight as he takes in the winter wonderland. He motions at someone behind him and out steps a man, much shorter than Stephan, wearing a cloak.

"Demetrius." My breath fogs out in front of my face as it laces with the arctic air.

"There it is," my dad mumbles, staring at something near the shoreline just in front of his feet, a blur of colors and shapes.

I focus like I've been taught to do and the colors and shapes alter into two figures that rise up from the ground, clutching onto each other for dear life.

"Oh my God." My heart stops at the sight I've seen before. Many times. In fact, pretty much every time I pass out.

I throw my hand over my mouth and start to back away. This is what my father erased to create a new path for the world. This is what was going to happen? Alex and I were going to die to save the world. I painfully understand now, what this means and what it means if I choose the right path.

I watch in torment as Alex brushes the vision form of me's hair from my face. "It'll be okay," he whispers softly.

"How do you know?" she says, tears streaming from her eyes.

"Because I do." Then he kisses her with so much passion that it electrifies the air. He keeps kissing her, his hands traveling all over her body as she grips onto his shoulders, fully welcoming the kiss, yet she's scared. The electricity intensifies and then finally Alex pulls back and hugs her against him tightly, whispering something in her ear that makes her skin drain of color. But then she says something else that looks like it means everything to her. And as she buries her face into his chest, a light brightening around the two of them, she appears content.

I shield my eyes, trying to see what's happening. I've never gotten past this part in my dreams, but deep down I know why. It's the same reason why when Alex looked in the future mirror, he only saw light.

Because it's the end for both of us.

"This is what happens right before the portal is about to open... the two of them stop it from happening, by sacrificing their own lives?" my father whispers under his breath as the light dims away. The sun shines brightly from the sky and the snow is melted, the land soaked with the afterglow. The Death Walkers, Stephan, and Demetrius are gone and ash is scattered across the ground and floating through the air. Everything is burned except for Alex and the vision form of me sprawled on the grass, our fingers intertwined as we lay side by side, dead.

My father shakes his head, tears rolling down his cheek. "I'm so sorry for letting this happen to you." He steps toward our bodies, crouches down, and reaches for us, preparing to erase us like I did to myself on the shore.

I start to sob uncontrollably. "This is what I have to put back," I choke. "I have to let this happen. Let Alex and me die, so that the world doesn't freeze over and everyone dies."

It's the most difficult decision I've ever had to make. Either I can walk away and let the world head to its frozen death or sacrifice Alex and mine's life so everyone can live. How can I do it? How can I kill Alex and myself?

"I can't do this," I whisper through my tears.

But as my father's hand hovers above Alex, I realize what kind of person I am, a life changing moment that will define me forever.

My hand trembles as I reach for my father. "I'm so sorry," I whisper then place my hand on his shoulder. He vanishes with a flicker and I collapse to the grass and cry until all the energy drains out of me. Then I curl up into a ball and for once, wish I was still emotionally numb.

Chapter 32

I wake up at the house, slamming to the floor, but don't open my eyes, even when everyone rushes to me. I can't do it—can't face him, so instead I let him carry me to the sofa, pretending I'm unconscious, while Alex stokes my back.

I hate to hear him worried like he is, but opening my eyes means I'll have to explain what happened. I'll have to tell Alex that we are going to die in the close future and that what I changed back was our deaths.

I'm not sure how much time goes by, maybe hours, as I stay that motionless, listening to them worry, knowing that eventually I'll have to officially wake up and tell them what I did.

"Gemma." Alex's breath feathers against my ear as he leans down and in desperation, whispers, "For the love of God, please just wake up."

His plea tears at my heart and I decide it's time. Opening my eyes, I sit up and he leans back to give me room.

"Oh, thank God." Aislin presses her hand to her heart, relief sweeping across her face as she sinks down on the coffee table. "You're okay, right?" She's been crying, eyes red and swollen.

I can't look Alex in the eye so I focus on Laylen and Aislin. "Yeah, I'm fine."

"What happened?" Alex asks, trying to catch my eye. "Did you change it or did something... bad happen?" He thinks I'm upset because my dad turned out to be evil. Part of me wishes that was the case.

I smash my trembling lips together, sucking back the tears, and manage to nod my head once.

He hooks his finger under my chin and forces me to look at him. "What's wrong? I can tell something's bothering you."

"I stopped him from changing the world's future." I release an uneven exhale. "So now it's back to what it was supposed to begin with before my father messed with it."

"So everything's good." Alex is deciding whether he should be happy or not. "The world's not going to end? In ice? My father's not going to get what he wants."

I squeeze my eyes shut and suck in a deep breath. "That's not all."

He's hesitant. "What else happened?"

Knowing I should tell him first, I open my eyes and ask Aislin and Laylen, "Can you two give us a second? I need to talk to Alex alone."

They give me lost looks at they get up and do what I ask. Laylen looks like I've wounded him, probably because he thinks I'm keeping secrets from him.

After the room is cleared, I turn to Alex and gather every ounce of courage I possess. "What I had to erase... what I had to allow to happen... what was originally supposed to happen is that... we... we sacrifice ourselves and die, killing the star with us."

He doesn't utter a word. The clock ticking. The wind howling. And I can hear Aislin and Laylen upstairs talking.

"So we say we love each other," he says with indifference. "And then we die and that's that."

I nod, unable to speak.

More silence goes by and then Alex abruptly gets to his feet. "I can't do this," he mutters and then storms out of the room and out of the house, slamming the front door behind him and it rattles the entire house.

Seconds later, Aislin and Laylen come rushing into the room.

"What happened?" Aislin asks, looking around. "Where the hell did Alex go?"

Telling them is less difficult but still hard. When I'm done, Aislin runs up to her room sobbing hysterically. Laylen stays with me in the living room, but sits quietly with his arms folded.

"So that's how it's going to happen," he finally asks in a quiet voice. "It doesn't seem fair."

"I'm not sure it really is either," I say, wondering if it's a selfish thing to say or not. "But it is what it is. No more changing things, not when I know that it'll lead to something good."

He drapes his arm around my shoulder and hugs me against him, kissing the top of my head before resting his chin on it. "Maybe we could fix it... Maybe we can do something else that would keep you guys alive."

Shaking my head, I shut my eyes and clutch onto his shirt, telling myself to hold on and not fall apart. "There's nothing we can do. Everything is back to the way it was supposed to be and changing it will only cause more problems and mess up things." Even though I try to fight them, the tears start to flow and I'm not sure if I'll ever be able to stop them.

***

In the midst of my crying, I somehow fall asleep and end up in my room. I recognize the familiarity of my bed when I start to wake up. My eyes are so puffy I think about not opening them again, but then I feel the hum of the electricity and make myself fully wake up.

Alex is lying beside me, not asleep, staring at me. "Sorry, I was just..." He looks a bit guilty.

"Watching me sleep," I finish for him, turning on the lamp. It's not completely nighttime yet but dark enough that I can only see the outline of him. I want to see all of him, savor the moments with him and everyone I care about.

"It's not as creepy as it sounds," he says, starting to laugh, but the happiness deflates quickly. He looks exhausted, dark half circles under his eyes, hair a mess, clothes wrinkled.

"No, it's pretty creepy," I attempt to joke, but fail miserably.

"You don't have to do that." He rolls onto his back and stares up at the ceiling. "You don't have to pretend that everything's alright when it's not."

"Don't I?" I whisper. "It hurts too much not to pretend."

He rolls to his side again and lets his finger travel down my cheekbone to my jawline, finally residing on the hollow of my neck. "Never pretend with me, Gemma. Promise me you won't. Promise me you'll tell me what you're really feeling no matter how bad it is."

I gaze up at his eyes that use to be so cold, but now give me so much comfort I can barely comprehend it. "You really want to know how I feel right now." I ask and he nods. I wet my lips with my tongue and then lean up, knowing that what I'm doing might be wrong, but it's what I want to do at the moment.

Without any hesitation, I press my lips to his and kiss him intensely but deliberately. I expect him to stop me and give me a big lecture about how we should stay apart, that we should let the star survive as long as we can. But he doesn't and we both decide just to live in the moment. Live for the now. Live to live because any other way wouldn't be right.

As he kisses me back with passion, he conceals his body over mine, his arms slipping upward and bearing his weight and my head is trapped between his arms. He's touching all of me but it doesn't feel like enough. I want more, but when I rush to rip of his clothes, getting caught in the heat of the moment like we've done so many times, he stops me by catching my hand.

"Just enjoy it, okay," he utters softly with fear in his eyes, like he's afraid to do so himself. When I nod, equally as terrified, he leans back down and kisses me gradually but with so much intensity, I swear we're going to burn the house to the ground. I can barely get air into my lungs as our tongues entangle and our bodies weld together, conforming flawlessly. The kissing goes on forever, longer than I knew kissing could go on for. When he finally pulls back, he strips my clothes off me, going slowly and not tearing the fabric and I do the same to him, my chest heaving as I gasp for air, feeling things I've never felt before. I try to bury them, knowing I need to restrain what I'm certain is developing inside me, and toss his shirt aside. Then I gently trace my fingers along his perfect chest and impeccable stomach, feeling his muscles flex under my fingertips. He lets me study him, feel every part of him, then he lays me back down and does the same to me, his fingers drifting from my face, to my neck, my breasts, then to my thighs, his mouth trailing after his hand and leaving a path of heat all over my skin. By the time he's done, I'm gasping for air and my body is aching for him to be inside me.

He must sense it to, because he situates himself between my legs and covers his body back over mine. "I want to say so many things..." he looks so torn. "But I don't think I can."

"You don't have to say anything at all," I whisper, leaning up to kiss him. "I already know."

He kisses me deeply as he thrusts inside me and my fingernails dig at the flesh on his shoulder blades as overwhelming passion, lust, want, and need consume me. For a moment I feel whole. At peace. Like I've done everything I've wanted to do. And as he rocks inside me, whispering, "Everything we'll be alright," part of me believes him.

Chapter 33

After having the most intense sex ever, I lie in bed beside him, face to face, staring at him, trying to brand his beautiful face into my mind so hopefully when I die, it'll be the last thing I see.

"You know, I never stopped thinking about you," Alex says, resting his hand on my hip. "After you left."

"I wish I could have thought about you," I admit. "But I didn't really think about much of anything honestly."

"It's not your fault," he says, tracing circles on my hipbone.

"I know, but I still wish I could have."

It grows quiet between us and then he sits up in the bed and reaches for his jeans on the floor. "I want to do something," he says and when he sits back up he has a knife in his hand. "I want to make another Blood Promise."

"What kind of a Blood Promise?" I sit up, intrigued.

"One that will help us through this." He touches his finger to the tip of the knife and pricks it. "One that will make the impossible possible."

I don't quite understand, but the silent plea in his eyes is enough for me to easily give into his request. "Alright, let's make a promise." I lift my hand that is marked with the scar of the original Blood Promise and hold it out to him.

He slices the palm of his hand open, his breath faltering as he carries my gaze and the carefully cuts mine. With blood trickling out of both our hands, he presses our palms together. *"EGO spondeo vos ero totus vox,"* The words pour out of his soul. *"EGO spondeo EGO mos operor quisquis capit ut servo vos."*

When he's done, I wait for him to tell me what he needs me to say, but he lowers his hand to his lap and puts the knife on the nightstand.

"That was a one-sided promise." I cup my hand to catch the blood but the wound is already healing up.

"It was a one-sided promise that needed to be made."

"But that doesn't seem fair... I didn't promise you anything back."

"Trust me," he says with a sad smile. "I got everything I needed."

Something about this is all wrong. "Alex, I—"

"Please Gemma, this is what I need," he begs and I surrender to him, because really I have no other choice.

Chapter 34

After a good night's rest, I decide to go tell my mother what's going on, mainly because I want to inform her that my father wasn't evil like she said, that everything he did was for her.

Alex is still fast asleep in my bed, so I quietly get dressed and slip out of the room so I won't wake him. When I get to Sophia and Marco's room where my mother is imprisoned, I sit down on the floor in front of her and stay calm.

"I saw what happened," I tell her, tucking my legs underneath me. "Dad didn't want to be like Stephan. Stephan marked him with the Mark of Malefiscus and he had to do what Stephan said—he didn't have a choice in any of it."

Her eyes widen as she scoots toward me. "That can't be true."

"But it is," I say, trying to read if she's lying. "He had to do it. He had to change the vision and it all happened because he wanted to be with you."

"He just wanted to be with me?" Her hands fall lifelessly to her side, her skin draining of color.

"I changed it back," I inform her, knowing that she could tell Stephan, but that it doesn't matter anymore. "The vision he changed to end the world, I changed it back so it's not going to happen... all is saved." I'm not sure what comes over me, but I lose it and start bawling. I crawl toward my mom, disregarding that she has the Mark of Malefiscus on her arm and wrap my arms around her, seeking comfort from her like I'm a child.

She puts her arms around me and gives me what I need. A loving mother, but I'm not sure if she's playing the part or really being her. Either way, I take it.

We remain that way until the sun rises and lights up the room. Then I pull away and explain to her why I'm crying. My voice sounds hollow as I speak, detached.

"That's what he erased?" she asks after I'm finished and my tears have dried. "He erased your death and in return the world would end."

"I think, either way, I probably would have ended up dying, but this way it's just Alex and me that die. And we take Stephan and all the Death Walkers down with us." I force a tight smile. "Which is a good thing, right?"

She grabs my hands and suddenly her eyes are filled with tears. "You listen to me, Gemma Lucas, you are not going to give up that easily."

"I—I'm not giving up," I stammer, stunned by her shift in attitude. "It's what happens. I can't do anything about it."

She swiftly shakes her head. "There are always loopholes."

"You always say that, but it was a vision—the only loopholes are to do what dad did and try to change it to something else, and all that will get me is a one-way ticket to being trapped in my own mind forever and I'll probably fuck up the future of the world again."

"There are always loopholes, Gemma," she repeats, taking me by the shoulders and looking me straight in the eye. "Think about it. Your father took you into the Room of Forbidden, where no one's supposed to enter. You got me out of The Underworld, which isn't supposed to be possible. Your soul is reconnected, which was never supposed to happen. All those things were caused by loopholes." She pauses. "Just because you saw your death, doesn't mean you have to die... I'm not saying that what you saw won't happen, but that you need to find your loophole through your death...make it so you survive after the star's power fades away."

"I don't know Mom..." I look at her with wariness.

"Do not give up. I want you to go into your room and read through that Foreseers' book—find your loophole. Promise me, Gemma. Promise me you won't give up."

"Okay, okay, I promise." I put my hands up in front of me and back away from the frantic look on her face, not believing that there's a loop hole, but figuring it won't hurt to look.

I go back into my room and Alex isn't there. He ends up being in the shower. So I climb into bed and start reading the Foreseer book. I'm only about half-way through it when I put it aside because I'm starting to get a headache. What I need is a quicker way to read through all this information and start to wonder if maybe Aislin knows a spell that can give me speed reading ability.

I shut my eyes and allow my brain focus on seeing a loophole. I'm not positive if I'm doing something wrong, but I have to try.

As I attempt to push my brain beyond the boundaries of seeing something that probably isn't supposed to be seen, I feel an explosion inside my skull. My vision spots before I fall off the bed.

Chapter 35

I end up on my side in the sand, the smell of the salty ocean air gracing my nostrils. When I open my eyes, the first thing I see is a pair of black boots.

"You can't cheat your way there," someone says. "You're going to end up in trouble."

I lift my gaze to my father, leaning over me, his violet eyes conveying worry, his long silver robe trailing behind him in the sand. "I think I already am."

"If you want to find out the answer," he says. "You have to search for it on your own, not take shortcuts."

I roll onto my back and shield my eyes from the sunlight. "Am I in your head again?"

"So you discovered where I am?" Displeased, he offers me his hand to help me up and I gladly take it.

I look at the horizon and then around at the seemingly endless beach with no sign of life. "Wait. Why aren't we in the same place as the last time I ended up here?"

"We are wherever I need us to be." He starts down the shore, leaving footprints in the sand.

I hurry after him, sand building between my toes and the ocean rolling up over my feet. "I thought you were in the Room of Forbidden? I thought you were stuck in your own head and couldn't get out, so how can you change places?"

He halts near a cluster of rocks and faces me. "I get bored sometimes and change the scenery to help pass the endless time." He begins walking again toward the rocks.

"Why didn't you just tell them what happened?" I ask as I rush to keep up with him. "Why didn't you say that Stephan made you change the vision because he marked you with the mark?"

He glances at me solemnly. "It's the downfall of being a Foreseer, Gemma. There are no second chances or room for mistakes. What's done is done and I won't ever be forgiven or trusted again for what I did." Silence passes between us as we reach the rocks and we start to climb up them. I want to ask him if he has evil blood inside him, but I fear his reaction and the answer so I remain silent.

When he gets to the top of the rocks, he gazes out at the endless ocean, the wind blowing through his hair "You need to stop worrying about me," he says as I stand beside him. "You have other problems to deal with at the moment."

"Like saving the world..." Pain resonates inside my chest. "I think I already did that... dad I was able to fix the vision you erased... I erased you before you erased Alex and me"

"I know you did," he says gloomily. "But that is not what I'm talking about."

"Then what are you talking about?" I wonder. "Because it always seems like you're talking in code."

"I'm telling you about what you're in store for." The bottom of his robe flaps in the wind. He hasn't looked at me since we got up here, staring at the sunlight, unblinking and I wonder how it isn't hurting his eyes. "What waits for you in the near future."

"I know what it is." My voice is off pitch, revealing the shakiness within me. "I know that I die."

"You're still not getting it." He blows out a frustrated breath and then looks at me. "You need to push that aside, otherwise you'll never be able to save the world."

"But I already did that. What more could I possibly do?"

He reaches into the pocket of his robe and retrieves a glistening silver ring embellished with violet gems that outline a massive lavender stone. He takes a hold of my hand and drops the ring into it.

The gems shimmer as I stare down at the ring. "What does it do?"

"I can't answer that," he says, turning toward the shore again and heading down the rocks.

"Why do you always say that?" I climb down the jagged rocks, still holding the ring, afraid to put it on because I have no idea what it does. "How can you give me things like this? And the mapping ball, but you can't tell me how to use them? And how do you even have these things if we're inside your head?" I reach the sand. "It makes no sense."

"This is my loophole," he explains, drowning in sadness and regret. "I'm able to give you these things, because we're in my head and not in the real world. What I do in here doesn't matter out there. But I can't tell you how to use them, since that would be interfering with what you need to do out in the real world. You have to figure out the answers for yourself and pave the world with your memories." He takes my hand holding the ring and encloses my fingers around it. "This is your loophole."

"My loophole to what? Saving my life or saving the world?" I rush to say as the ocean begins to bleed away into the sand. The sunlight dims almost as if night has fallen and it grows quiet. "Wait, don't send me back yet. I have a ton of questions."

"No more trying to cheat, no matter what happens," he calls out as I float backward, my feet lifting up from the sand. "If you're not careful, you'll end up in here."

I shout at him to please tell me as the ocean vanishes and becomes one with the sand. Then I'm ripped away back to my room. When I open my eyes, though, I'm not in my room.

I'm engulfed by light, just like when I die.

Chapter 36

"You're not dead," someone says as I turn in circles, searching for something other than light. "If that's what you're thinking."

An eerie chill slithers up my spine and at the same time my sense of smell is attacked by the scent of flowers and rain. "But you're dead."

"Am I?" the tricky half-faerie teases. "Are you sure about that?"

I clutch onto the ring as I strain my eyes to see through the light. "I'm not sure about anything anymore."

I hear a thump then footsteps moving through the light in my direction. "Of course, you're not. You've been clueless from day one. In fact, you're the most clueless girl I've ever met. You're always looking for the answers in the wrong places."

"That's not true," I say as he materializes right in front of me, his golden eyes inches away from mine, his body so close I'm instantly suffocated with his body heat.

I step back. "You're dead... aren't you... and so am I."

"I'll answer that shortly," he says with a wink. "But right now you have to go back." He strides toward me and shoves me backward, his hands searing hot against my shoulders. I scream as I tumble into darkness.

***

I bolt upright, gasping for air. It takes a minute for me to realize I'm on my bedroom floor, safe and sound from any potentially dead faeries. But what kind of detour was that? I mean, some strange things have happened while I was traveling around with my Foreseer power, but that... that was too much.

I get to my feet with the ring that my father gave me still in my hand and then head downstairs to tell everyone what happened. I find Alex in the kitchen, making a sandwich. His hair is freshly wet and he's wearing jeans with a thermal shirt. Laylen is at the kitchen table, flipping through a magazine, and dressed as if he's about to go out to a Goth club.

"I have to tell you something," I announce and then it all comes pouring out of me.

"Why does he keep giving you things without an explanation of what they are?" Alex asks when I'm done, taking the ring from me and studying it closely.

I'm sitting on the countertop with my legs dangling over the edge. "He said it was because I had to figure things out on my own and pave the world with my memories, whatever the hell that means." I take the ring back and run my finger along the gemstones. "It's not like I can pave them with too many, since my time's about up."

Alex chokes on bite of sandwich. "No it's not," he says, catching his breath.

"Alex, I don't think it's good to deny it," I say. "I think it's better if I—"

He strides toward me, positioning himself between my legs and concealing his hand over my mouth. "I'm not going to let you say that." He lowers his hand from my mouth to my thigh. "I won't let you give up yet." He leans in and softly brushes his lips against mine, then pulls away and says, "Laylen and I have to go somewhere right now, but we'll talk about this more when we get back."

Laylen glances at his watch. "Is it time to go already?"

Alex nods with his gaze fastened on mine as he backs toward the back door. "Yeah, we should get a move on if we want to make it."

"Where could you two possibly be going?" I ask, hopping down from the counter. " And together?"

"Just somewhere," Laylen says, giving me a smile, but it's a mask to hide something else—his uneasiness.

"Don't worry." Alex reaches for his jacket on the back of the kitchen chair. "We'll be back soon."

Before I can say anything else, they walk out the door, leaving me stunned and standing in the kitchen alone. It's so strange, the two of them walking out of the house together. And content. It makes me worried.

Finally, I decide to find Aislin and ask her if she knows what's going on. I find her in the living room, sorting through spices and various bags of what looks like pixie dust, a bowl in front of her where's she's mixing ingredients.

"Do you know where Alex and Laylen are going?" I ask, stuffing the ring into my pocket and then joining her on the sofa.

She glances up from a plastic bag filled with flakes of orange leaves. "They went somewhere *together*?"

I nod, hitching my finger over my shoulder toward the back door. "They just left."

She opens the bag and sniffs it. "Okay, that's probably one of the strangest things I've heard all day."

"Maybe." But I'm not sure that it is. I think seeing Nicholas might top it. I sit back down on the couch and tighten the elastic in my hair. "So have you figured out what went wrong with your spell?"

She shakes her head, sealing the bag back up. "It's strange but from everything I've read, it should work. And I can feel the power, but when I try to use it, I get nothing but this fizzling feeling." Aislin opens the laptop in front of her. "I think maybe we could—"

A loud bang from inside the house silences both of us.

"What the hell was that?" Her eyes are huge as she looks at the window and then at the front door.

"Maybe Alex and Laylen forgot something." I start for the kitchen and she tensely follows after me.

Bang. Bang. Bang.

Aislin whispers as we approach the kitchen, "It's coming from in there."

"Do you have a weapon, just in case…" I trail off as smoke rounds the corner of the kitchen, snakes around my ankles, then heads for the living room.

Aislin grabs a knife from the pocket of her hoodie. "Ready when you are."

I don't have a weapon, but decide to rely on my strength something I need to get used to. "I'm ready."

We swing around the corner on high alert and step into the kitchen. The smoke is coming in from a roaring fire burning in the garbage can in the driveway and the back door is agape, swinging in the wind and letting the smoke and wind inside.

Aislin lowers the knife. "Oh, thank God. For a second I thought the house was burning down."

I inch toward the back door. "Yeah, but who started the fire and opened the door?"

She raises the knife again as if this has just occurred to her. "You think something's wrong?"

"I'm not sure."

The sight of the fire blazing toward the night sky is sending red flags popping up all over the place. My mind drifts to a vision I've never seen before yet it feels like I have and I wonder if it's some kind of after effect from changing a vision. *Fires in the street. Chaos everywhere as vampires, fey, werewolves, all paranormal creatures run the streets wildly under the control of evil.*

You need to prepare yourself.

I remember something Stephan once said to me; how he was told that Alex and I might kill the star and ourselves and ruin his plan but that he was working on an alternative plan. But what does that mean?

"Do you have a fire extinguisher?" Aislin asks, checking the cupboards and drawers.

I point at the cupboard below the kitchen sink. "It's under there."

Moments later, Aislin is outside and putting out the fire. I watch from the back steps, holding her sword, assessing the very quiet neighborhood around me. Everything seems normal, but something still feels off.

We head back inside, locking the door behind us and Aislin sets the extinguisher down on the kitchen floor. "There. Fire problem all taken care of."

She goes back into the living room while I put the extinguisher back in the cupboard. "Something's not right," I mutter, feeling the calm before the storm. "I can feel it."

Chapter 37

It seems like hours tick by as I wait for something else to happen. It gets later, then earlier as morning starts to arrive. I'm not sure what compels me to do it, whether its sheer bravery or stupidity, but I finally dare to but the ring on. I expect something to happen—a big explosion or maybe I disappear—but nothing happens. So I keep it on and lie down on the sofa, skimming through the Foreseer book, while Aislin works on a spell.

At about three or four o'clock in the morning Laylen and Alex finally return. I sense something is immediately off by their bloodshot eyes and their worn out expressions.

"Are you two okay?" I ask as Alex shucks off his jacket and hangs on a coatrack it in the foyer. "Have you been crying? Or are you stoned?"

Alex chuckles under his breath. "I promise we're fine." He doesn't really answer my question, though, swinging and arm around my shoulder and guiding me with him as he goes into the living room. He smells like barbeque sauce and beer, which makes me wonder if they went to a bar.

Laylen lies down on the sofa, looking beat, and I catch Aislin giving him a look that begs him for the details of where they've been, which he ignores, shutting his eyes like he's going to take a nap.

As I'm about to sit down, Alex tugs me in the other direction toward the stairway. "Hey, come with me for a minute. There's something I need to talk to you about."

"Okay." Something is up.

"You put that thing on?" he asks, unexpectedly alarmed as he taps the ring on my finger while we gradually make our way upstairs.

I run my finger along the gems. "I wanted to see if it would do something if I did, but it didn't."

He seals his lips together, probably shoving down a lecture and remains that way until we're in my room. He shuts the door behind us and even though it's dark, he doesn't turn the light on. Then he stands by the door and I can't see what he's doing, but I can tell he's thinking about something intense by the way the sparks nip and bite at my skin.

It starts to drive me crazy, so I flip the light on. "Okay, fess up. Where did you and Laylen go?" I lie down on my bed on my stomach and rest my chin in my hand, fixing my attention on him.

He shrugs, his relentless gaze locked on me. "I just needed to talk to him about something."

"So are you two friends again, then? I really hope so because this jealousy, male testosterone thing between you two is getting old."

He chuckles under his breath then lies down on the bed beside me on his back. "Yeah, I guess it was getting old, wasn't it." He drapes his arm over his head, gazing up at the ceiling.

"It feels like you're keeping something from me," I state, turning my head and resting my cheek on my hand so I can look at him better.

"No, it's not bad. It's good…everything will be alright."

My heart misses a beat. Those are the words he whispers to me right before we died. "How do you know that for sure?"

"I just do."

"Alex." I move a pillow out of my way and scoot closer to him. In response, he puts a hand on my stomach, just under my shirt, and his fingers splay across my stomach. Something warms inside me, in a different yet equally—maybe even better—way than it normally does, but the sensation baffles me. "What did you say during the Blood Promise you made to me last night?"

His expression is unreadable as he grabs my leg and swings it over his midsection. "I'll tell you tomorrow, okay? But right now I just want to lay here with you and do something else to get my mind off the end of the world."

I look down at my leg over his and then my eyes glides up his body and meet his tired gaze. "What did you have in mind?"

"I just want to have normalcy for a bit." His arm wraps around me, his hand pressing on the small of my back, and he pushes me closer to him. "Just for a second." He pauses then utters, "I won't let it happen." he says it more to himself than to me as his fingers trace the length of my spine. "I'll never let anything happen to you."

As his hands slide up to my shoulders and our bodies align, I'm not even worried about dying. And when he kisses me, every worry I have diminishes. I once heard this song or maybe it was a saying about letting yourself die in a blissful, loving, perfect moment, so that you could die happy. I think I might feel that way right now.

Chapter 38

I wake up to an empty bed and have a cold feeling residing deep in my bones. I feel wired, like my peaceful dream has rejuvenated me. But as the reality that I can't feel a single drop of sparks in my body sets in, I start to panic.

I get out of bed to go looking for Alex. The house is quiet and I assume everyone is asleep. As I step into the hallway, I notice right away that something isn't right. Not only can I feel no presence of Alex, I can hear a heart beating from somewhere nearby. At first I think it's my own, but as I press my fingers to my pulse, the rhythm doesn't match.

I notice that there's a light on downstairs, so I go down there, the heartbeat moving with me. There's a lamp on in the living room, but the sofa is empty and the kitchen to the side of me is dark.

I start to turn away, but something catches my eye. There's an envelope with my name on it sitting on the coffee table. My stomach drops as I pick it up, tear it open, and take out the paper inside it. I think part of me has an idea of what it is before I read it and this sickening feeling builds in my gut and the unknown heartbeat starts to give me a headache.

Gemma

I know you may not understand why I have to leave, but I need you to try. I don't believe that your end comes when you think it does. I believe there's another way, and I'm going to do whatever it takes to find it—find a way to save you. But I can't do it while I'm around you. I can't keep hiding what I feel, but if I let it all out and you end up feeling the same way, then I know it'll be the end for both of us. And I can't let that happen.

I will always save you, no matter what. And I need you to hang on until I do.

Yours forever,

Alex

The letter slips from my fingers and floats to the floor as I hunch over, gasping for air. My stomach aches, like a kick to the gut.

I will always save you.

How can he leave me? I can't live without him. I realize that now. It hurts so badly that I think I'm going to throw up and I think I might just lie down and die. But then something dawns on me and I stumble up the stairs, still hugging my stomach, and barge into Laylen's room.

He jumps out of bed, kicking the blankets off as I turn the lights on. "What are you doing?" he asks, rubbing the tiredness from his eyes.

"Please tell me you didn't know." I beg, walking toward his bed. "Please tell me that's not why you guys left the house."

He's apologetic expression says it all. "I'm sorry."

"But you're supposed to tell me stuff like this," I say, shaking my head trying not to cry. "That's what we do—we help each other out."

He sighs, throwing the blanket off himself. He's shirtless and usually I ogle his lean body, but not this time. Things have changed—I have changed. I can feel it inside me, through the pain in my stomach, through the nagging prickle in the back of my neck, and the heart beat that won't stop. "I couldn't tell you this." He pats the bed for me to sit and I do so, even though I'm still upset. "He needed to leave... it was too hard for him to keep turning off what he felt for you. And if he stuck around, he worried you'd kill each other and nobody wants that to happen. This is for your own good even if you can't see that right now."

"But he thinks he can find a way to save me and I think it's a lost cause."

Laylen draws me to him and kisses my forehead. "You never know. Maybe he will... And I sure as hell hope he does."

I trace the fresh wound on the palm of my hand as my heart shatters into pieces. I see where Alex is coming from, but it doesn't make the empty void inside my heart feel any better.

He left.

And I might not ever see him again.

"Do you know what he promised me?" I ask.

"He promised you everything would be alright and maybe it will." He pauses. "He told me to keep an eye on you, while he was gone. And make sure nothing happened to you."

"I don't need to be watched," I say, upset. "I can take care of myself."

"Yeah, you can, but you're also precious cargo," he says, forcing a playful tone. "And precious cargo needs to be taken care of."

"I'm not precious cargo. I'm destructive. Without me, there would be no star, and therefore, there would be no problems."

He leans back so he can look me in the eye. "That's why he told me to keep an eye on you. He didn't want you to sink into this sad pit of despair because he was gone. He has this theory that even though you guys aren't supposed to be close because of the star, he also thinks that separation is bad for you... that it makes you feel like something's missing, drains your energy, and makes you depressed."

"Because of the star?"

"I'm not sure."

I shake my head as hot tears spill down my cheeks. I can't hold it back anymore, so I lean my head on Laylen's shoulder and cry until I'm too exhausted to keep my eyes open. Then Laylen carries me back to my room as I drift to sleep, dreaming of fires, stars, and the heart beat that won't stop flowing from inside me.

Chapter 39

A loud bang rocks the house and wakes me up from a dead sleep. There's an orange glow coming from outside my window and my bedroom door is wide open, the hallway suffocated by darkness. I'm not sure how long I've been asleep, but I am guessing for an entire day and well into the next night.

As another bang echoes through the house, I quickly get out of bed, noting the separate heart beat is still haunting me. As I peer out into the hallway, I notice the door to where my mom is staying and the window is open, the curtain flapping in the wind.

I rush into the room, then trip back at the sight of the empty chains on the wall. "No, how did she..." She escaped, somehow, and got out of the window.

I'm about to go peer out when I get whiff of the scent of flowers and freshly fallen rain. I slowly turn around and step back, folding my arm across my stomach.

"You're dead," I say, backing away from Nicholas.

Nicholas leans causally against the doorframe, raising his eyebrows "Am I?" He matches my move-ments, taking two steps for every one I take, and closes the space between us quickly. When my back hits the wall, he stops in front of me, looks down at his arms and body and says, "Wow, I look really good for a dead guy."

I shake my head as my pulse races wildly while the other heart beat inside me calm. "This can't be happening."

Nicholas rolls his eyes. "I think you always kind of knew I wasn't dead. You saw me for God sakes." He knocks his fist on the side of his head. "Come on Gemma, think."

"But that was a nightmare," I say in an uneven voice as I inch sideways toward the window.

"Was it?"

"It was in my book."

He rolls his eyes again, his playfulness draining from him. "I guess technically I shouldn't be here, being dead and all." He shrugs nonchalantly. "Yet here I am."

"So you're dead?" I brace a hand on the bedpost to keep from collapsing to the floor as my stomach starts to burn. "How can I still see you then?"

His grins. "Just another amazing thing about you, I guess."

"This is the last thing I need right now. An annoying faerie ghost haunting me," I snap through gritted teeth, the burn becoming almost unbearable. "Why the hell are you here?"

"Because you changed the vision," he says, stuffing his hands into the pockets. "And that brought me back."

"But I changed it back to what it was supposed to be to begin with."

He narrows the space between us and I start to stand up and move back, but he takes my arm and makes me sit down on the bed, not roughly like I expect. "Not *that* vision. The other one where I was supposed to take you to Stephan. I'm sure you've been noticing that things have been a little off and out of order right?"

"But I…" I seal my lips together, feeling as though I am going to throw up. "I didn't mean to mess things up… I just didn't want Alex dead…. And I thought I was helping the world by changing the other vision."

"Doesn't matter—you still did it. And now you're responsible for my death. If it wasn't for you changing events, I would never have been in that car to begin with. And now you're stuck with me."

My eyes widen in terror as I hunch over, gasping for air. "This can't be happening."

"Don't worry." Nicholas crouches in front of me so we're at eyelevel. "I'm not here to hurt you. I'm here to help you."

"You left the note on my bed, didn't you?" I ask. "And you were that annoying talk-show-host voice too?"

He nods. "It was the only way I could communicate with you."

"But why? Why help me now?"

"That's another story for another time."

I let a breath ease from my lips. "Why can I see you now? And when you're dead?"

"Because you're wearing this." He touches the ring on my finger and I flinch. "It's the *orbis of silent* or ring of the dead. It gives you the power of seeing the dead."

Why would my father give this to me? How is seeing the dead my loophole?

Nicholas sits down beside me and I cringe from his closeness. "You have such a bumpy road ahead, and you don't even know it," he says, his gaze flickering to my stomach and then to the chains on the wall.

"Do you know where my mother went?" I ask.

"Perhaps." He motions at the window. "You can look out there, though, and find out for yourself." When I hesitate, he urges me by giving me a gentle push on the back. "Go ahead and look for yourself. Go see the damage you've caused, Gemma Lucas, the girl who destroys everything."

Taking a deep inhale, I get up and go over to the window, my knees wobbly and my palms covered with sweat while vomit burns at the back of my throat as I peer out.

Garbage cans burn in the streets and fires light up the sky. At the next house over, a vampire is drinking from a woman's neck in the front yard, right out in the open, as if it didn't matter, as if all the rules have changed.

"What did you think was going to happen?" Nicholas asks as I back away, putting my hand over my mouth because I'm fairly sure I'm about to puke. "That you could change events and everything would be okay? That you could mess around with visions and everything would be fine?"

You need to prepare yourself. The brief vision I saw was a warning.

"Why would this happen just from me changing one event of my life?" I motion at the window where fires blaze and screams flood the streets. "How could it lead to all this destruction?"

"Don't you remember the butterfly effect?" he asks. "This all happened because I never handed you over to Stephan that day; therefore he had to work harder to try and capture you. He started igniting the Mark of Malefiscus on the followers of Malefiscus, something he was going to do when the portal opened, but he did it sooner so they can help him capture you. And thanks to Stephan and his memory tampering abilities, they think they've been born with the mark." He nods his head at the window where outside in the street a witch is attacking a helpless man with sparks of fire flying from her hands. "They think this is the way things are supposed to be."

"Can we fix it?" I brace my hand on the wall to stop from falling over. "Can we make all the madness stop... make things better?"

"Perhaps." He looks at the ring on my finger. "But right now every single creature marked with the Mark of Malefiscus is roaming the streets." He grazes his finger across the mark on his forearm. "My mark is useless, though, since I'm dead."

"I'm going to fix it," I say in a trembling voice. "No matter what it takes... even if I have to die sooner."

The corners of his lips quirk as he eyes my stomach. "You sure you're strong enough to take that risk, even in your condition."

I put my hand on my stomach and I swear to God the heart beat grows louder, stronger. "What condition?"

"Oh you don't know yet." He's enjoying himself way too much. He steps toward me and reaches for my stomach, but I jerk back, which makes his eyes flash with anger. "You're choices aren't just your own anymore," he says.

I look down at my stomach as what he's saying clicks. "No… it can't be… it's not…" I shake my head in denial, the room swaying as reality slaps me across the face hard. "I can't be pregnant."

He laughs, but it's rough and raw. "I guess I should be saying congratulations."

Tears pour out of my eyes as my legs give out on me and I buckle to the floor. I press my hand to my stomach and listen to the heart beat and the fires and screams just outside, wishing desperately that Alex was here.

Jessica Sorensen is a *New York Times* and *USA Today* bestselling author that lives in the snowy mountains of Wyoming. When she's not writing, she spends her time reading and hanging out with her family.

Other books by Jessica Sorensen:

Shattered Promises (Shattered Promises, #1)

Fractured Souls (Shattered Promises, #2)

Unbroken (Shattered Promises, #2.5)

The Secret of Ella and Micha (The Secret, #1)

The Fallen Star (Fallen Star Series, Book 1)

The Underworld (Fallen Star Series, Book 2)

The Vision (Fallen Star Series, Book 3)

The Promise (Fallen Star Series, Book 4)

The Lost Soul (Fallen Souls Series, Book 1)

Darkness Falls (Darkness Falls Series, Book 1)

Darkness Breaks (Darkness Falls Series, Book 2)

Ember (Death Collectors, Book 1)

Connect with me online:

jessicasorensen.com

http://www.facebook.com/pages/Jessica-Sorensen/165335743524509

Jessica Sorensen

https://twitter.com/#!/jessFallenStar

Broken Visions